MONTANA MAVERICKS

Welcome to Big Sky Country, home of the Montana Mavericks! Where free-spirited men and women discover love on the range.

The Tenacity Social Club

In rough-and-tumble Tenacity, it seems everyone already knows everyone else—*and* their business. Finding someone new to date can be a struggle. But what if your perfect match is already written in the stars? Pull up a bar stool and open your heart, because you never know who you might meet at the Social Club!

Superwealthy rancher Daniel Taylor didn't even know he wanted love until he walked into Mike Cooper's bar, but now Mike is all he can think about. The down-to-earth cowboy/bartender is unlike anyone Daniel's ever met, and he wears his heart on his sleeve. But Mike's also raising his eight-year-old nephew, and he doesn't think he belongs in Daniel's upscale world. Maybe they were never meant to be more than a fling, but Daniel can't bear to walk away...

Dear Reader,

This is my first time writing in the Montana Mavericks world, and what an honor it is to welcome you back to the miniseries, as well as to Tenacity's ongoing mystery!

Daniel Taylor wasn't planning to be in Tenacity at all, let alone stay for a spell in the hardscrabble town. His truck has different ideas, and when it breaks down on the side of the highway, the Tenacity Social Club—and gorgeous bartender Mike Cooper—is an unexpected refuge. Buckling under the expectations of his family's mega ranching business, Daniel is floored by how much comfort, friendship and passion he discovers with the local rancher.

Mike quickly tumbles head over heels for Tenacity's newest visitor, especially after seeing Daniel bond with Mike's young nephew, Cody. But though much brings the pair together, familial and emotional barriers threaten to tear them apart. I hope you enjoy their journey of finding true love in Tenacity. Getting to usher Daniel and Mike's happily-ever-after into the world has been a true privilege.

If you're interested in other Montana-based books I've written, as well as a few other Harlequin Special Edition novels with LGBTQ+ characters, my website (laurelgreer.com) has info, extras and a link to my newsletter. You can also find me on Facebook or Instagram. I'm @laurelgreerauthor on both.

Happy reading!

Laurel

A MAVERICK WORTH WAITING FOR

LAUREL GREER

MONTANA MAVERICKS

Special thanks and acknowledgment are given to
Laurel Greer for her contribution to the
Montana Mavericks: The Tenacity Social Club miniseries.

Harlequin®
MONTANA MAVERICKS

Recycling programs for this product may not exist in your area.

ISBN-13: 978-1-335-14321-1

A Maverick Worth Waiting For

Copyright © 2025 by Harlequin Enterprises ULC

For questions and comments about the quality of this book, please contact us at CustomerService@Harlequin.com.

 Harlequin Enterprises ULC
22 Adelaide St. West, 41st Floor
Toronto, Ontario M5H 4E3, Canada
www.Harlequin.com

Printed in Lithuania

MIX
Paper | Supporting responsible forestry
FSC® C021394

USA TODAY bestselling author **Laurel Greer** loves writing about all the ways love can change people for the better, especially when messy families and charming small towns are involved. She lives outside Vancouver, BC, with her law-talking husband and two daughters, and is never far from a cup of tea, a good book or the ocean—preferably all three. Find her at www.laurelgreer.com.

Books by Laurel Greer

Montana Mavericks: The Tenacity Social Club

A Maverick Worth Waiting For

Harlequin Special Edition

Love at Hideaway Wharf

Diving into Forever
A Hideaway Wharf Holiday
Their Unexpected Forever

Sutter Creek, Montana

From Exes to Expecting
A Father for Her Child
Holiday by Candlelight
Their Nine-Month Surprise
In Service of Love
Snowbound with the Sheriff
Twelve Dates of Christmas
Lights, Camera...Wedding?
What to Expect When She's Expecting

Visit the Author Profile page
at Harlequin.com for more titles.

For Shellee. The very best village, heart, laughter, safe space. I really need to send a thank-you card to whoever designed that sunset driver's license.

Chapter One

Daniel Taylor rested one wrist on the steering wheel and one arm on the open window ledge of his pickup. The two-lane highway through eastern Montana was straight, flat and deserted enough that he could've put the vehicle in cruise control and taken a nap without incident, but driving like this didn't put him to sleep. The early May sun glinted pale gold off the fields on both sides of the road, stretching into infinity.

Roads like this signified possibilities, and this one, in particular, stretched toward the state line where he planned to do some real-estate reconnaissance. Damn, he was itching for something to light him on fire. Branching out from Montana, finding a spread in North Dakota with his brother would spice things up enough to no longer be on a slow, monotonous slide into middle age.

The Check Engine light flashed for a second, then went out. *Weird.* A loose wire?

He'd take a look when he stopped for gas before the border. He had hours of driving ahead of him. Hours of dreaming. Time and space to dwell on possibilities without a hundred human-resources fires to put out at the Triple T Ranch. In a different family, he might get away with treating his Director of Training and Employee Development title like a courtesy, but the Taylor legacy hadn't been built by people who'd taken advantage of their last name to slack off and let other people do their work for them.

Taylor men care for the people they love by working the land, son.

If only he felt as connected to that legacy as he had when he'd been younger.

The warning light blinked again. *Hmm.*

Should he stop?

A road sign stood out against the endless fields. Five miles to Tenacity.

Five miles to that bar.

That smile.

That easy, engrossing conversation, hours that felt like minutes. He'd replayed it like a script in his head, over and over as winter had turned to spring.

He shook his head. His moment in time in the Tenacity Social Club, months ago but still so fresh, was safest left in the past.

He *was* looking for something but wasn't about to find it in a small, struggling ranching town. And "something" wasn't a bartender more than fifteen years younger than Daniel.

Though…

He'd consider it on the way home. A quick stop after dealing with his business across state lines. Say hello to the man whose laugh was impossible to erase from his mind. Relive a sliver of the snowy, winter afternoon when he'd stopped to stretch his legs on his way home from another long trip.

Mike had been special. Unforgettable, if Daniel allowed himself to be sentimental, which—what better time to luxuriate in old memories than a long, quiet drive?

Unfortunately, even the most intriguing hazel eyes he'd ever seen couldn't prevent intrusive thoughts from rising.

As much as his life working for his family's beef empire had brought him wealth and status, neither was something he could define as *his*. His dad and uncles still had a firm grip on the place. At forty-four, it was beyond time he woke up in the morning and felt like more than a cog in the massive Taylor machine. Money could buy some surface-level happiness, but it didn't fill a person's heart and soul.

He'd thought it was enough. He'd been raised for it to be enough, to see it as his life's purpose. But with four of his five siblings paired off with people they adored in the last year and a half, and their children and stepchildren bringing extra layers of love to their lives, the fulfillment he'd always found at Taylor Beef seemed hollow. At least Seth, his brother closest in age, was still a romantic holdout. He was interested in a new property venture with Daniel, and it seemed the prime time to explore. Daniel knew he was beyond fortunate to have the means to do so.

His father and uncles had always just assumed the boys in the family would follow in the footsteps of their elders. Not only did Daniel regret not challenging the ingrained gender roles and the impact on his sisters to the degree he should have, he'd led the way for his two younger brothers to get pulled in without questioning other possibilities. Over a year ago, he'd admitted at the Thanksgiving dinner table that if he'd had the choice, he would have picked a different career. He couldn't shake the curiosity of where he might have ended up if he'd pushed back against family expectations.

He, of course, loved his mom and siblings. Hearts of gold, all of them. And he wasn't going to hold his breath, but maybe one day his dad would get his head out of his ass about Daniel's life outside of work.

The Check Engine alert lit up again, and this time stayed on.

He wasn't going to panic. His truck was close to brand new, so the warning was probably for a finicky sensor in need of a reset.

Still, he'd be best off stopping somewhere with the equipment to read the diagnostic code. Maybe he'd stop in Tenacity today after all. The town was tiny, but there had to be a mechanic somewhere—

The engine went silent.

His dash illuminated like a fairground midway.

He let out a word best left in the cattle yard and eased the truck to the side of the road.

What the hell?

He groaned. The Temperature Warning light hadn't gone off, no weird exhaust… Battery, maybe? Or—*crap*—the alternator. Why it would be faulty on a truck he'd bought last year, he didn't know, but it wasn't something he could fix on the side of the road.

He got out and checked under the hood, but nothing showed up to change his best guess about the mechanical culprit.

Glancing east, he estimated it was two or three miles to Tenacity, then checked his phone. Signal was strong, thankfully. After finding a number online, he dialed the mechanic and connected with a kind receptionist. He explained his predicament.

"Well, now. I'd love to tell you we can respond right away, but Chuck's out on a call, which'll be an hour or so at least. And his daughter's home sick." Her gum chewing reminded him of walking through a muddy field in rubber boots, but her compassion sounded genuine. "Hell of a day to need a tow, hon."

Even with the sun shining, he had no desire to sit on the side of the road and twiddle his thumbs for hours while he waited for Chuck to finish up his to-tow list.

"All right, then. I suppose I'll walk into town, find somewhere to pass the time. Chuck can call my cell when he's brought the truck in."

In fact, he knew of just the place. A basement establishment with dim lights and decades of initials and hearts carved into the worn wood of the bar. Hopefully complete with a gorgeous bartender who could absorb the words of a weary traveler with a wink and a pour.

He threw his leather duffel over his shoulder, made sure he hadn't missed any visible valuables and then started hoofing it toward the hardscrabble town.

Damn, it was warm for May.

He'd already folded his blazer and slung it over his bag.

The second button of his dress shirt was the next thing to go.

Then his sleeves, rolled up to the elbows.

He was about to strip the shirt off and saunter into town in his white undershirt—he doubted anyone in Tenacity would care, as he didn't remember it being the kind of place with dress codes or business casual expectations—when he saw the dilapidated population sign.

He would never have predicted he'd end up here again. Tenacity was a world away from Bronco and Taylor Beef, from dinners with his mother's crystal wineglasses and porcelain plates and his father's confused comments whenever Daniel's sexuality got brought up.

You still seeing men, son? I thought you would have grown out of that back in college.

Of course, Thaddeus Taylor wouldn't know who Daniel was dating, given he rarely brought his partners home to dinner. He rarely dated anyone long enough to justify them meeting his family, anyway. Beyond introducing a man to one of his siblings now and then, his dating life and his Taylor obligations didn't intertwine. Life was simpler if he kept everything separate.

Finding someone who was okay with his boundaries wasn't always easy. In fact, the last time a man had caught Daniel's eye had been in this very bar. He'd been hit by an undeniable attraction—the rush of recognizing the magnetism of the person in front of him. He craved another hit of it.

With a blister forming on his right heel and cotton sticking to his back, he finally made it to the main drag. The stairs with the arrow leading to the basement bar were only a block away.

He caught a glimpse of himself in a window. Yikes. *Disheveled and sweaty* was not his best look. His stomach flipped. He didn't want to know what his hair looked like or how red the hatband mark on his forehead would be.

Maybe it would be best to change plans and hit up the diner across the street. But then, he'd miss the chance that Mike might be on-shift...

Nah, he'd leave his Stetson on and hope the bartender was unfazed by dusty, road-weary cowboys.

The possibility was enough to get his booted feet jogging down the stairs, blister and all.

He slid off his sunglasses and stuck them into the front pocket of his shirt. Doubt crept in with each step. Mike saw hundreds of faces a week. What were the chances he was going to remember Daniel's after so many months?

The lights were dim after being out in the sun, the room dominated by shadows. Behind the bar, broad shoulders and a head of errant curls caught the overhead lights. Strong hands were busy wiping the counter.

Familiar lines, despite the passage of a few months.

Daniel crossed the floor, eyes adjusting.

He was a few feet away from the mouth-watering stretch of a worn, gray T-shirt emblazoned with Captain America's shield when Mike looked up from his task. He flashed the brightest smile Daniel had ever seen in his life.

Well, the brightest he'd seen since the last time he'd sat down on one of those worn stools.

"Danny? You're back?"

Danny. Right. The bartender had shortened his name the

last time, too. Why was it so charming? No one ever referred to him as Danny. Usually Daniel. Occasionally Dan. His mom still got away with *peanut,* which was ridiculous, but he didn't dare correct Imogen Taylor. And his gut was telling him not to correct Mike, either. Tenacity was the kind of town where a "Danny" moseyed up for a beer. Real life didn't have to exist here—not until Chuck the Mechanic called.

Daniel slid onto a stool. His feet thanked him, but the rush of excitement from Mike's cheerful welcome was even more of a panacea. "Surprised to see me?"

Mike rubbed the back of his neck and ducked his head a little. "Well, yeah. I did not have you showing up at my bar on my bingo card for today."

"I didn't have my truck breaking down on mine, but…"

Mike braced his arms on the bar.

Daniel's mind went a little blank.

"But?" Mike prodded.

"*But* I think I'm okay with the change, given I get to catch up with you." He normally wouldn't be so forward with someone he barely knew, but Mike had mentioned being gay when they'd talked during Daniel's last visit.

Mike's smile widened and his cheeks flushed. "I— It's good to see your face. What can I get you?"

Daniel ordered a draft lager.

"Beer's on me," Mike said, sympathy mixing with the gold in his eyes. "Dealing with a mechanic's bill is no small thing. My truck broke down a few years ago, and it took me months to pay it off."

Daniel's chest tightened at the honesty—and also at the difference in their situations. He could walk onto a car sales lot, buy three trucks with cash and hardly make a dent in his bank account.

But not only would pointing that out make him sound like a hell of a prick, the sliver of financial anonymity felt good.

The Taylor name made for a more-than-comfortable life, but it had a habit of getting in the way of real connections. Money both pulled people in and pushed them away.

He'd leave his last name out of the conversation for a while. Mike seemed to genuinely like "Danny."

Daniel nodded and sipped his beer. "Yeah, with luck this one won't be too big, but from the pattern of the lights flickering and then all of them going on after the engine died, I'm guessing it's the alternator."

Mike winced and passed him a bowl of pretzels. "Ouch. Labor on that won't be small."

Lifting a shoulder, he smiled. "Might have fixed it myself if I was at home, but it wasn't happening on the side of the road. I'm good to cover my beer tab, though, as much as I appreciate your generosity."

"You walked all the way in from the highway?"

"I've heard one too many cautionary tales about hitchhiking to hop into the cab of some stranger's truck." Even though he was tall and able to defend himself, he never wanted to be in a situation where he had to. It was safer to keep his guard up in new places or certain familiar places he knew weren't as open to his romantic orientation. He'd been out since he'd been twenty, but decades of navigating often-conservative circles, as well as his own father's prejudice, had made him cautious.

"I wish you'd had my number," Mike said. "You could have called me for a lift. So long as you don't consider me a stranger."

The bartender's hands had stilled on the pint glass he was polishing, and his lips parted a little, emphasizing how full they were.

Soft. Edible, even.

Clearing his throat, Daniel said, "No, I don't consider you a stranger."

Bright hope filled the other man's gaze. "I'm glad to hear that."

Not a stranger, but what was he? Even after their long conversation months ago, Daniel didn't feel he knew Mike well enough to call him a friend.

Yet.

Still a lot of hours left in the day, and no sign of his truck being finished. He got the impression from the bartender's welcoming demeanor that most people walked away from the Social Club feeling like they *had* made a friend.

Then again, I wouldn't mind more *than friends.*

"I read the book you recommended," Mike said. "The fantasy one set in Southeast Asia? I couldn't put it down."

Daniel blinked in surprise. Mike had a hell of a memory, it seemed.

They fell into easy conversation. Deeper than small talk. Daniel ate up the opportunity to learn about the sweet, fascinating man. Picking up on his mannerisms, too, filing them away as teeny revelations worth knowing. The little tug of teeth on his lip whenever Daniel managed to earn a laugh. A dark curl falling across a friendly gaze. With every teased-out fact about Mike—an inability to say no to a plate of wings, how he filled his thermos with tea instead of coffee in the mornings, the claim he'd spent more of his childhood on a horse than on the ground—Daniel wanted to learn more.

"It doesn't matter how many times I watch *Inside Out*," Mike said, leaning in like he was ready to confess something dear. "I cry at the Bing Bong part every time."

"Can't say I've seen it," Daniel said. "Not much opportunity for cartoons. But I did well up when I saw *Lord of the Rings* in the theater. Having a world I'd pictured in my head for so long come to life…"

"Exactly," Mike said. "It's all about imagination. Though I didn't need an imaginary friend when I was a kid—I had my twin, Maggie. We were terrors. The number of times my mom caught us balancing on the cross beams in the barn…"

He chuckled and turned his arm over, showing a thin scar zigzagging from his wrist to his elbow. "She was right to be pissed off by how badly I broke my arm when I took an inevitable fall. Didn't get to go swimming in the creek all summer. Didn't get to whine about it, either, given it was my own damn fault."

"I did something similar once," Daniel admitted. "Slid off the roof of one of the outbuildings and broke my ankle when I was fifteen. Couldn't help with fall roundup. Thought my dad was going to disown me."

He checked his watch. It was after three. The mechanic must have towed his truck to the shop by now. If it needed a new battery, he could take care of that, drive back to Bronco tonight and try again in the morning. If it was the alternator, or something else, it might be easier to stick around here and wait instead of doubling back.

Maybe Mike would be free for dinner.

Before he could ask, the front door swung open. A sliver of daylight beamed in from the outside staircase, catching the chestnut glints in Mike's curls.

Mike's face lit up, too.

A ball of sheer energy bounded into the room. The young boy dropped a backpack onto the floor and crossed his arms on the edge of the bar, nearly hanging off the worn wood.

With tousled brown hair and freckles across his pale cheeks, the kid was a miniature Mike, minus the outdoorsy tan.

Holy crap.

Was his cowboy crush…a dad?

Chapter Two

Mike braced himself, well used to his nephew leaning against the bar to recount his day. Today's tale was no different—a wave of "Guess *what*" and then a torrent of the grade-school politics dominating the playground at Cody's small elementary school.

Cody's well-being had been a big part of Mike's life since his twin sister had delivered a healthy son eight years ago. Maggie's boyfriend at the time hadn't wanted anything to do with fatherhood, going so far as to change colleges to escape his responsibility. Mike and his parents had been the opposite, supporting Maggie's choice to be a mom, and being her support system ever since. Being an uncle meant being a father figure, and he was more committed to that than anything else in his life. Especially since Maggie had left for a one-year international-development job back in the fall.

The work opportunity was a big sacrifice on all their parts, but with how passionate Maggie was about maternal health, Mike had barely stopped to think about his answer when his sister had floated the idea of her working in South America for a year. She'd volunteered for month-long stints in the past and could do so much more with a longer, paid term of service. With Cody being older now, he understood why his mom was away. And Mike was so damn fortunate to have the time to care for and bond with his nephew, who was growing and changing daily.

For the couple of days a week when Mike worked afternoons, Cody usually barged into the Social Club and waited with Mike until five, when Mike's mom got off work and would swing by to take Cody home. So long as Cody wasn't sitting on one of the bar stools, which were the only seats where alcohol was permitted in the afternoon, the boy was welcome in the popular gathering place. He typically sat in the office, or more recently, occupied a table nearby. Mike usually fed him a snack while he did homework or read whatever new paleontology book the school librarian had put aside for him. Nor would he be super out of place once the usual crowd of high schoolers arrived to hang out until around dinner time. Afternoons at the club with Cody were some of Mike's favorites. Not much beat listening to his nephew deliver his post-school-day report.

Today, though, the handsome cowboy sitting to Mike's right, staring into a half-full beer, was stealing Mike's attention.

It had been months since those strong hands had gripped a glass on Mike's bar. He'd never expected to see Danny again. What else was he supposed to think when the guy had taken a phone call and then disappeared?

Danny's abrupt departure from his first visit hadn't stopped Mike from thinking about him since, though. He felt like he could spend the rest of his shift teasing out information about what made Danny tick and wouldn't even come close to knowing all the things he wanted to know about the man. Those dark eyes, busy examining the carbonation in the golden brew, pulled at Mike like industrial magnets. How was it possible to be that handsome? Mike felt the crooked smile all the way to his marrow.

He shook his head. He needed to focus on his nephew, who

was bouncing on the balls of his feet, going into detail about knowing all the spelling words of the day. His twin was depending on him—he'd promised her he'd be extra present for her son while she was a continent away.

Mike poured a small milk for Cody to take to his table and slid the glass across the bar to his nephew before allowing himself to glance at Danny. The other man was the picture of insular focus, doodling his finger along the initials and hearts carved into the bar.

Daniel's other hand was white around his pint glass.

Hmm.

"So *then*," Cody said, "there was this soccer game at recess… Me and my team were winning, but Bianca got a ball to her *face*, and her nose was super bloody! It got in her *teeth*."

He could tell his nephew couldn't decide whether to be awed or disgusted.

"Poor Bianca. I bet it hurt a lot. Embarrassing, too," he said.

In the corner of Mike's vision, Danny knocked the last half of his drink back and put the empty glass down with a *thunk*.

"Sorry for the unexpected turn into blood sport," Mike said, turning to his guest.

"All good." Danny's wide gaze flicked between Mike and Cody. "You—you've got your hands full here with your kid." The last word pitched up, almost a question.

Oh, hell.

"Wait. Danny. Let me introduce you." He reached across the bar and tousled the curls so like his own. "This is my nephew, Cody. My twin sister's son. The club's 'no minors' policy doesn't kick in until eight p.m., so some days after school he comes and hangs out until my mom finishes her shift. She's a nurse at the urgent care in Mason Springs."

The corners of Danny's mouth relaxed. "Your *nephew*."

"Yeah." Mike smiled back. "I don't have kids of my own. Or

a partner." Damn, maybe he'd misread what Danny was getting at… "I mean, not that you asked. But…yeah. I'm single."

Tied down, for sure, between working at the family ranch and moonlighting behind the bar and upholding his promises to Maggie, but he didn't have any romantic entanglements.

"Uh… Want another?" Mike motioned to Danny's glass.

"I'll take a Coke, please." Danny's shoulders were still stiff. His rolled-up sleeves exposed tense forearms, muscles highlighted with shadows. He shot a careful smile in Cody's direction. "What, uh, what grade are you in, Cody?"

"Third grade. Almost fourth. Next year, I get to be in intermediate and be a big buddy and get letter grades and use a binder and have a *desk*."

Danny's eyebrows rose. "Important stuff, binders and desks."

"Instead of sharing a table," Mike explained as he wielded the fountain gun. The guy's reaction suggested it had been a while since he'd contemplated the ins and outs of the primary grades. The fact he'd thought to include Cody in the conversation at all made something swoop in Mike's chest.

"Of course," Danny said, accepting a freshly fizzing soda from Mike. "So you babysit? Or is it something more permanent?"

"I get to live with Uncle Mike for a hundred and seventy-four more days," Cody broke in with the confidence of an only child well used to being in the company of adults. "My mom's working far away, until Thanksgiving. With moms and babies. She's helping them stay healthy. And we get to talk to her on Zoom *twice* a week. And I get to sleep at Uncle Mike's and hang out with him and Grandpa and Grandma. And help with the horses on weekends. And *sometimes* the calves, when they're little."

Danny's shoulders relaxed a fraction. "I used to pitch in with my dad and uncles when I was your age, too."

"Oh, my dad's not around. But Grandpa and Uncle Mike

show me all sorts of stuff. Grandma, too, but she's busy being a nurse, so she's not as much of a rancher."

Mike chuckled. Nothing about Cooper Ranch would run if it weren't for his mom being the most organized person he knew. "It's Grandma's world, Cody, and we're all just living in it. She keeps us all in line."

"She's the best." Cody took a drink of his milk, leaving a white stripe on his upper lip. "She takes me to the library a lot. We've started reading Percy Jackson, and I got a prize for finishing all the books they have on dinosaurs. Uncle Mike and me are working on a dinosaur diorama as big as the *kitchen table*."

He held his arms out as wide as they could stretch.

"Wow." Danny looked to Mike for confirmation.

Mike shook his head and held his hands eighteen inches apart. He'd become a decent crafter since last November, but nothing of the three-foot-plus scale.

"It has *real plants*," Cody explained. "And a giganotosaurus and an amargasaurus, because those lived close to where my mom is living right now. I made them out of papier-*masshy*."

"Mâché," Mike corrected gently.

"Do you have a favorite dinosaur?" Cody asked Danny.

"Can't say I do," Danny said, "but I bet you have a whole list of good candidates."

"Uh-huh. I mean, carnivores are the best, but…"

Mike had to give it to Danny. The guy listened and nodded to the pros and cons of Cody's favorite reptiles with serious intent. It took more than five minutes before Danny's eyes started glazing over.

"…not that a styracosaurus and an allosaurus could *really* fight, because the styracosaurus was from the late Cretaceous period and the allosaurus was from the Jurassic period, but man, it would have been *so* cool, and—"

"A stellar lineup, as always, Code," Mike said, steering

his nephew from part two of his impromptu session of Dinosaurs 101.

"The *late* Cretaceous period." Danny sounded a little stunned. "What a neat fact."

Cody grinned. "Thanks."

"My nieces are still really little," Danny said, "but maybe when they're your age, they'll be as smart about this stuff as you are. *Though,* my step-nieces and -nephews are older. The next time I see them, I'll have to ask them if they've ever learned about styracosauruses."

Mike softened at the other man's kindness. Danny looked like he'd been hit by a whirlwind, but he wasn't sloughing off Cody's enthusiasm like so many adults did.

"Do any of them play piano?" Cody said. "*I* can."

He bounced away from the bar, across the empty dance floor to the beat-up instrument donated years ago by a local and often used by their live artists. With careful fingers, he plunked out the melody to a simplified, one-handed version of "Moonlight Sonata."

Danny let out a breath that sounded a lot like, "Holy crap, I'm overwhelmed."

"He's high energy," Mike said, pouring another round for the only full table in the place and leaving it on a tray for the college-age waitress to deliver.

"Don't apologize."

Mike half smiled. "I wasn't. I wouldn't change a single part of him."

"Good," Danny said. "A boy needs to hear those kinds of things from his loved ones."

Years of bartending kicked in, a red alert. Either Danny had been showered in positive messaging as a kid…or the very opposite.

The tension pulling the man's mouth taut suggested the second.

"That's the goal," Mike said. "My parents and I have to fill a big hole with Maggie gone. But working internationally is one of her dreams, one we wanted her to make happen."

"That's pretty amazing."

He lifted a shoulder. "Is it, really? I get to pour glasses of milk in addition to beer, and listen to Beethoven on repeat, and learn way more than any human needs to know about dinosaurs."

"It's more than that," Danny said quietly.

"Sure, but… It's family." He smiled. "Are you close to your nieces and nephews, Danny? Or any other kids?"

He shook his head. "My sister Charlotte works in a different town, and between than and how busy my job keeps me, it's hard to carve out quality time to see her stepkids or her baby. Same for my sister Eloise, who has a toddler. We struggle to get our schedules to line up."

Mike tried to imagine not being close to his sister and parents and couldn't. He also wasn't naive and knew he was fortunate. Not every family was as loving as the Coopers, and more than one thing Danny had said hinted he might not come from the same strong bonds as Mike.

Danny's phone buzzed on the bar.

"The mechanic?" Mike asked.

"Looks like it. I'll take this outside."

Mike's chest tightened and he clenched the soda gun. A spray of Sprite hit the edge of the small sink, splashing back onto his T-shirt and apron. He cringed and dabbed at the mess with a bar towel.

Danny's brows shot up. "You okay?"

"Yeah. Just…say goodbye before you leave this time."

The other man's lip twitched. "I didn't realize you were interested enough to warrant a goodbye last time."

"I was."

Danny's dark eyes glinted as he turned. He headed for the door, phone to his ear.

Mike took a deep breath and finished cleaning up the sticky drink as best he could. A goodbye would mean Danny was gone, and Mike didn't want the man to leave at all.

Daniel jammed his cell back into his pocket and glanced around Tenacity's main street. A few restaurants and shops, and along the sidewalks, the occasional tree with bright, spring-green leaves. Not Bronco, but somewhat charming in a run-down way. It was the kind of place where it felt like the asphalt was mixed with half tar, half hard work.

And thanks to the mechanic's jam-packed schedule this afternoon, Daniel wasn't going to be able to escape anytime soon.

He *could* do the responsible thing and ask someone to come get him. He wasn't super close to home, but it was still drivable in an evening—he could call in a favor from a friend or one of his siblings.

Seth would be champing at the bit to reschedule all the appointments Daniel was supposed to attend with the North Dakota Realtor tomorrow.

Or...

He glanced back at the entrance to the Social Club.

Or he could reschedule those appointments himself and *not* call for a ride.

His hand was yanking on the street-level door handle and his boots were on the stair treads before he could register what he was doing.

Sidling up to the bar for the second time today, he rested an elbow on the surface. "Hello again."

"You came back," Mike said, voice light with surprise.

Happiness rushed through Daniel. Mike wanted him here. He could make some sort of easy joke about his truck making the decision for him, but in reality, he *was* choosing to stay. Easiest choice he'd made in a long while.

"Wasn't going to walk out on you twice."

"I'm glad. Gotta admit, I was disappointed when you left without warning last time."

"I'm sorry. I didn't think. Got called home for an urgent work matter." Even so, Daniel wasn't sure how he *had* managed to walk away months ago. What *had* he been thinking?

"Where *is* home?" Mike asked.

Nowhere Daniel wanted to mention at the moment.

"Hundred miles or so from here." He cleared his throat. "Too early for a whiskey, isn't it?"

Mike frowned. "Depends on how bad the news about your truck was."

"It isn't bad or good yet. He's guessing the alternator, but won't get the chance to confirm until tomorrow, and then suspects there will be a delay for parts, being it's the weekend."

"Dang, I'm sorry."

I'm not.

"It'll delay my trip to North Dakota, but que será, será, right?"

"The future's not ours to see?" Mike said.

Daniel grinned. "You know the song? My grandmother used to sing it to me."

"Mine, too." Mike's smile was soft.

When it came down to it, Daniel liked the possibility of staying in Tenacity for an extra few days. Seth could rein in his impatience over the property hunt. When was the next time Daniel would be in Tenacity with free time and the ability to get to know Mike? Fate was dropping an opportunity into his lap. He'd be a fool to turn it down.

"So, uh, there wouldn't happen to be a hotel within walking distance, would there?" he asked.

"The Tenacity Inn's close by. Nothing fancy, but it's clean," Mike said. "Want me to call ahead for you?"

"Sure."

Mike pulled his phone from his pocket and tapped the screen a few times.

Man, he was a good guy, through and through.

So much so, Daniel might need to be cautious. The younger man had *caretaker* written all over him. It hadn't taken long to figure out how much Mike did for his family, the crowning piece being his guardianship of Cody.

For all intents and purposes, Mike was a full-time dad. Couldn't get much further from Daniel's wheelhouse than parenthood.

Daniel shook his head at himself. He was thinking about being in town for a couple days and maybe having a drink or two with the guy. Yet another casual connection, like he was used to. Not anything resembling commitment. Getting nervous about it was beyond silly.

Mike disconnected his call and turned back to Daniel. "Carol—my godmother—is on the front desk tonight and has a room for you. She'll even cut you a deal, given you weren't expecting to need to stay."

"Kind of her," he said. Unnecessary, but kind. "Do I turn left or right at the top of the stairs?"

"Head west," Mike said. "Unless you were serious about that whiskey."

"Tempting," Daniel said, "but I'm in dire need of getting cleaned up after my walk along the highway."

"Rain check, then."

Damn, Mike's smile was contagious. Daniel caught himself grinning wider than Cody had when he'd been in the middle of his dinosaur intensive. "You got it."

Chapter Three

The Tenacity Inn was a couple of blocks from the Social Club. Not far enough to get warm again, but enough to remind Daniel he hadn't dealt with the blister he'd earned walking into town. The woman who greeted him at the counter was tall and slim with dark brown skin. Her curly, pale blond hair was tight to her scalp.

"Well, now, you must be the man Mike called me about. Danny, right? A friend of his?"

He guessed she'd been doing her job for a long while, as a no-nonsense efficiency lay under her kind facade, the sort developed through years and years of greeting and managing guests.

"Friends. Yes," he replied, placing his duffel on the floor and pulling out his wallet. If Carol was Mike's godmother, he had no doubt anything he said could be held against him in a court of law, or at least over tea with Mike's mother.

Free from the distraction of Mike's conversation and strong shoulders, exhaustion started to weigh heavy in his limbs, the kind brought on by dealing with travel uncertainties. He was glad he hadn't asked Mike about meeting up again tonight. He wasn't going to be good company until after he slept off his day.

He handed over his platinum card. If only he had one that didn't advertise the size of his bank account.

She took it between two manicured nails. One dark eyebrow rose sky high.

"It works—I promise," he said.

"Hmm." Her gaze narrowed, skipping from his credit card to his dress shirt and Stetson to the leather duffel he'd put on the floor. "You seem like the sort of cowboy who would've passed Tenacity right on by were it not for your car troubles. Daniel Taylor, is it?"

He swallowed. It was a common enough last name. He hoped she wouldn't make the connection to his family and their expansive holdings. A few days of anonymity, of getting to still be "Danny" sounded terrific.

"Yes," he said simply. "And whether or not I'd have normally stopped in, I'm sure glad Tenacity was here, otherwise I would have had a hell of a walk to the next town over. Let's start with two nights, if you have the space."

She rang through his transaction and passed over a key card.

"Thank you, ma'am." He picked up his bag. "Is there a room service menu I might look over?" Making his way the few blocks back to one of the few restaurants in town was more effort than he felt like putting in at the moment.

"You're assuming we *have* room service, Mr. Taylor," she said with a wink.

"Just 'Danny,' please. And it's no problem if you don't. I can figure something else out."

"Shush," she said. "I'm just teasing a friend of my godson. We can order in from Pete's Pizza or The Grizzly. They deliver for our guests. Nothing as upscale as you might be accustomed to." Her smile was guileless, but her sharp gaze raked over him, making it clear she suspected he was used to life's finer offerings.

If he wanted to fly under the radar, he'd have to be subtle, starting with not showing any surprise over his limited din-

ner options. He wasn't going to complain. When in Rome…
or in Tenacity, rather.

"I'm partial to a burger," he said. "Any chance The Grizzly carries beef from Mike's family's spread?"

Loyalty to Taylor Beef or not, he liked to support local producers.

"I believe they do deal with Cooper Ranch. Pillars of Tenacity, that family." She paused. "Have you known Mike long?"

He felt his cheeks flushing. "Not particularly."

"Doesn't mean you haven't had the chance to get to know each other, but I have been accused of sticking my nose where it doesn't belong."

"Like any decent, self-respecting housekeeper—or desk clerk, in your case—you listen in on the other line?" he said, unable to stop himself from quoting his favorite Christmas movie.

"I wouldn't give me *that* much credit," she said with a wink. "But you have excellent taste in holiday musicals."

He laughed. "Glad you know that one."

"Know and love." She smiled. "Should I put in your burger order?"

"Please. I skipped lunch, so I'm liable to start eating the fake fruit, soon." He pointed to a decorative pyramid of wood apples.

"I'll make sure it gets to your room quick like a bunny, then." She motioned toward a hall on her left. "Second door on your right, Danny."

The hall's faded carpets and striped wallpaper threw him back to his mom's design choices from his childhood. She'd redecorated five times over since then, and looking at the dusty rose motif of the inn, he couldn't say he missed it.

Opening the door to the room, he tossed his bag onto the luggage stand and glanced around. Not much different in here. Pristine, smelling faintly of pine cleaner, but spare. Fussy, worn wood furniture and a television about the same vintage as the one he'd owned back in his college days. The welcome guide on the nightstand, a few sheets of paper clipped into a binder, informed him of his access to fourteen channels. Wi-Fi access was limited to the lounge area.

Chuckling—he needed to tuck his inner spoiled self away before he managed to insult someone—he settled in and waited for his dinner. He wasn't here to be pampered and didn't mind a quiet Friday night. He just needed his truck fixed, with the hopeful side benefit of getting to know Mike a little better. The inn was as good a mustering station as any.

"Best Saturday *ever!*" Cody had his arms spread like airplane wings—correction, pterosaur wings—and was flying circles around the island in Mike's parents' kitchen. Mike and his mom were putting sandwiches and cut veggies together, trying to avoid getting clipped by an eight-year-old's "wing."

Between work in the barn and out in the pasture, Mike had put in almost a full day already, and it was barely noon. Cody wasn't jazzed about the usual ranch goings-on, though. They had tickets to the rodeo tonight, and the barrel-racing lineup was one he'd been looking forward to seeing for months.

Mike spread mustard and mayonnaise onto a dozen slices of bread, then layered on the tomato his mom had sliced up.

Cody let out a loud *caw*—his best guess at a pterosaur's cry, no doubt—and narrowly avoided colliding with Ellen when she opened the fridge door to take out a jug of milk.

"All right, you." Ellen palmed the top of Cody's head, holding him in place. "Take your flight path into the backyard so we don't lose any glassware."

"Or come help me put the sandwiches together," Mike said, holding out a stack of lettuce leaves.

Sighing, Cody took the frilly pile and tossed a leaf over each layer of Mike's carefully arranged tomatoes.

"I know you're excited about the rodeo, but let's work on your accuracy there, kiddo," Mike said.

"But it's the Hawkins Sisters!" Cody's eyes were on the verge of being literal stars. "They are *sick*. Almost as sick as the bull riders. Maybe when I grow up I could be a bull rider."

"I thought you wanted to be a paleontologist, sweet pea," Ellen said.

"Yeah, and a pilot," Cody said. "Can't I do all of them?"

Ellen shot Mike a look telegraphing how much she hoped Cody didn't end up on the rodeo circuit. Thanks to her career, her injury-vigilance meter was set to *high*.

"You just keep exploring, Cody." Mike wiped his hands on a paper towel and then ruffled his nephew's hair. "Curiosity is the most important thing."

"You always say that." Cody bounced onto one of the stools tucked under the island.

"Because I'm smart." He put one of the sandwiches on a plate and put it and a glass of milk in front of his nephew.

"And you say that, too. And then you say I need to slow down, and Grandma says I need to think twice, but I don't know, because pilots and bull riders have to go fast."

"Not so much paleontologists," Ellen said. "They need to be meticulous."

Cody chewed his sandwich, a puzzled expression on his face. His mouth was still full when he said, "Huh?"

Mike's mom raised a grandmotherly eyebrow. "Chew and swallow so you don't choke. And *meticulous* means very careful. Which you have to be when you're unearthing fossils."

"I *know*, Grandma." Cody put his sandwich on his plate. "Yesterday I got to tell Uncle Mike's friend all about dinosaurs. He barely knew anything, so I made sure to explain which ones were carnivores versus herbivores, and which ones would win in a fight, and the eras when they lived and—"

"More bites, Cody," Mike interrupted. He was full up on

dinosaur lectures for the moment, nor did he need Cody talking more about the man who'd come into the bar yesterday. "You can come help me in the barn once we're done."

"Oh, man, I want to go to the rodeo *now*," Cody whined, dragging out the last word for at least three beats.

"Doesn't start until six," Mike said.

"Will Danny be there? Is that why you told him about the hotel? Because of the rodeo?" Cody asked.

"I doubt he'll attend, Code. He was only in town because his truck broke down. Didn't say anything about staying."

Cody turned to Ellen. "He was real nice, Grandma. I mean, besides not knowing much about the Cretaceous Era. But he said he used to ride horses and help with the calves when he was eight. And he liked the song I played on the piano, though I guess he might have just been being nice like grown-ups do sometimes. He talked a lot to Uncle Mike, too."

"Did he? Boring grown-up stuff?" Ellen asked mildly.

"Super boring," Cody said before finishing off his sandwich.

Ellen shifted her gaze to Mike. "You've never mentioned a 'Danny' before."

Mike lifted a noncommittal shoulder. "No one important, Mom."

Cody's jaw dropped. "That's mean, Uncle Mike."

Damn it. Mike raised his hands, palms forward. "That came out wrong, Cody. Sorry. I didn't mean Danny isn't a nice guy or anything, but we're not close. He's a customer, who happens to be kind."

And funny and hot and interesting.

Cody, seemingly placated by the explanation, asked to be excused and then zoomed off when given permission.

"Be ready to shovel manure in ten minutes!" Mike called after him, digging into his own sandwich.

"Lord, he reminds me of you at eight years old."

"He'll be asking me 'What time is it' and 'Do we get to leave yet' all afternoon," Mike lamented.

"Oh, no doubt. Are you not excited to go to the rodeo yourself?"

"Of course," he said, after he finished swallowing a bite. "It'll be a good show, and I assume I'll run into Jenna and Diego."

Mike had attended many a rodeo in Tenacity with his best friend, Jenna Lattimore, since she moved to town after college. Hell, they'd done everything together, as a trio with Rob, her husband, and Mike's other best friend. Rob's death had broken them both for a while, especially since Jenna had been pregnant when Rob passed. Stepping up while Jenna grieved had been Mike's sole choice, for her and her baby's sake. But time had passed, carrying them through the storm. The small joys in life, like going to the rodeo together—extra sweet now that Jenna had her daughter, Robbie, and her new fiancé, Diego Sanchez—seemed like a gift again. Mike was lucky to count them as family.

Having a good time with Cody and socializing with friends for a few hours would make for a banner Saturday night. But as soon as Cody had asked whether or not Danny was going to be there, the possibility had planted a flag in Mike's head.

"You know, Carol and I were chatting this morning. She said someone from out of town checked in last night and he happened to mention you," his mom said.

Curiosity surged at what Danny might have said.

He couldn't let his mom see *how* curious he was, so he let out a bland "Hmmm."

"Carol said he seemed like he was used to something with a much higher Yelp rating than the Tenacity Inn."

"I don't know him well, Mom. We've had all of two conversations." Though if Danny had actually complained about the simplicity of his lodgings, Mike would have been surprised. Nothing the other man had said yesterday implied he was picky about where he ended up for the night.

"Maybe he's from the city," Ellen mused.

Mike shook his head. "He has ranching experience. I think his family owns a spread. Got the impression he grew up on it."

"Might be true, but maybe he moved. He might live in a bigger—or richer—town than Tenacity now."

"Why does it matter?" Mike asked.

"Just a thought. If this man has caught your eye, it would be better if he came from a similar background. Easier to get along when you have things in common. You've learned that the hard way."

He waited for her to bring up a specific example off the too long list of men who'd proven he had less than stellar romantic judgment. The captain of the high-school football team had been a cliched and predictable mistake. The president of the Student Union in college had at least liked guys, but his New-York-finance-career dreams had eclipsed Mike's plans to stay in Montana. Same with a rodeo star who'd come through Tenacity. And his most recent ex, the one time he'd tried dating a rich man… Yikes. Just yikes.

So yeah, it was a relief that Danny seemed down-to-earth. Too kind and alluring to call *average*, but not flashy or out of Mike's league.

His mom, however, did not need to know the details yet.

"Who said anything about me showing interest?" he asked.

"The look in your eye gave you away," Ellen teased.

Mike groaned.

"No need to hide your feelings from me. You know I'm all about you finding someone to love."

"I know, Mom," he grumbled. "I'm not desperate, though. I'm twenty-eight, for God's sake."

"Twenty-eight and lonely," she said.

"Ouch." Sure, now she didn't hold back.

"You're so quick to tell your nephew to dream and to make sure your sister can reach hers, but make sure you're giving your own equal attention."

"This is my dream," he protested. "Working the ranch with Dad is fulfilling—I promise."

"And I'm glad for that. But it's okay to want company while you do it."

"Well, it's not going to be with a guy who's just passing through Tenacity," Mike said. "I can't let Maggie down, and I know how much Dad depends on me. And can you imagine what Jenna would do if I ended up with someone I had to move away to be with? Not likely, Mom."

She shook her head. "Michael, I wasn't saying anything about you going anywhere. I just liked the happy look on your face when Cody mentioned this man's name."

Mike knew more than his expression lit up when Danny was mentioned—his whole body did. And it was a feeling he wanted again and again.

Chapter Four

"You're where, dear? I thought you'd be in North Dakota by now."

"Tenacity, Mom. In need of a new alternator," Daniel explained while he fussed with the front of his hair, squinting into the mirror in desperate need of resilvering.

"Oh, no! What about your appointments with the Realtor?"

"Easy, now," he said. "It's an annoyance, not a crisis."

One he planned to take advantage of after spending his morning getting a timeline from the mechanic and unloading a few more personal effects from his truck. Thankfully he kept clean jeans, work shirts and boots in the crew cab for any time he needed to switch from office work to ranch work. He'd fit into Tenacity's vibe far more in denim and a snap-front shirt than the business-casual duds he'd packed for his real-estate dealings.

"But you and Seth have been mulling over buying a stretch of land for months now. I thought you were looking forward to setting eyes on some possibilities."

"I am." He was just looking forward to seeing Mike again more. "I'll still get there, Mom. I have a few extra days to play with. I took this whole week off."

Though his plans for Saturday were getting away from him. If he was going to clock some time flirting with a cute, younger bartender, he needed to finish getting ready and get over to the Social Club while it was still the afternoon slow period.

"Oh, Daniel. Always so reluctant to reach out," Imogen chided. "There's no need to be stranded when I can hop in the car and come get you."

"No, don't!" He cleared his throat. "Too much of a hassle."

She paused, no doubt over the emphatic protest. "We'd be home in time for a late supper. I could have Lina hold the lamb roast."

"There's no need. I won't starve here. The burger I had last night was delicious. I could go for another one." Or maybe he could catch a bite to eat with Mike somehow. Cody's company made things a bit more complicated, but Mike had mentioned his parents pitching in some nights.

"Why on earth would you want to spend a weekend in such a nowhere town?" She sounded beyond horrified. "There can't be anything to do."

"I'm sure I'll find something. I don't mind a couple of days to myself, to be honest. It's been a busy few months since Cattle Con."

The whole family had been caught up in a flurry of activity for over a year now. Aside from Seth and him, the rest of their siblings were focused on engagements and weddings, stepkids and babies. There was ranching for Ryan, of course—he hadn't escaped being shuttled into business and agriculture courses in college followed by a job at the Triple T—but their sisters were all rocking their jobs and businesses in other fields. Allison was climbing the ranks of her software firm in Seattle. Charlotte loved the ocean and had managed to stay immersed in her passion even in Montana, by working at the aquarium in Wonderstone Ridge. And after deciding Taylor Beef would never be the right fit, Eloise had built her own marketing firm. It was hard not to envy their success away from Taylor Beef. And with how quickly their generation had grown through marriage and engagements, it was hard not to be overwhelmed by all the differences.

But at the end of the day, things *weren't* different, not for him. He was still following the same path he'd always followed. He knew he wasn't alone in the feeling. Seth had expressed his dissatisfaction, too, hence them agreeing to find a side gig together. He still worried it wouldn't be enough.

"Hard work is important, honey," his mom said, "and I know more than anyone what the ranch costs us. It's okay to need a break. But I worry about you, all alone."

She sighed, as if she hadn't anticipated still feeling the urge to solve her kids' problems once they were adults.

And while he imagined parents worried about their kids for each tick of the clock marking their lives, he didn't want to be her source of stress.

"I date, Mom."

"I wouldn't know, given how rarely you've introduced me to anyone you're seeing."

"That's a big step," he said.

"You're *forty-four*. Between you and Seth, the number of questions I field from my sorority sisters—"

"Sorry to harm your image, Mom."

Silence stretched between them. "You're right. But it's easier to think about how it looks on the outside rather than admit my oldest son doesn't feel comfortable introducing me to the person he's interested in."

"Damn, Mom. It's less about you and more… Look. There hasn't even *been* anyone I've felt strongly about in a long time. I mean, I know I was with Greg for years, and I did bring him to family events. Where, I'll remind you, Dad pretended Greg was my friend from work, not my boyfriend. But dating someone at work ended up being a rotten idea after a while." He cleared his throat. "Do you think I don't *try* to find love?"

"Well, I'm not sure, Daniel—"

"I *do*. But there aren't a ton of eligible men in Bronco, and I can only get so close to someone when I meet them on business trips or vacations. It's just hard to meet Mr. Right, okay?" Harder still? Actually letting himself fall in love. It was a level of vulnerability he'd reached for, or at least *tried* to reach. Not that he'd ever succeeded. Man, that was hard to admit, even to himself. Easier to blame the lack of eligible men instead of all the times he'd chosen to break things off with a guy rather than open himself up to a deeper relationship. "Here's the thing. Even if I was serious enough about someone to bring them home, Dad still won't—"

What was the point in reiterating his father's flaws? She either saw it or she didn't.

She hummed, the sound edging on regretful. "I know I need to do better on your behalf, Daniel. So does your father. And after he made that asinine comment about you outgrowing being gay, I made him promise…"

"Promise what?"

She sighed. "Some things need to stay within a marriage, Daniel. But I won't stand for him refusing to acknowledge who you are. Please know that."

I'll take "Things I don't want to talk about" for four hundred, please, Alex.

"I appreciate you going to bat for me, Mom, but I refuse to chase after Dad, hoping for his acceptance. I mean, maybe there's still room for him to wake the hell up, but that's on him, not on me."

"I want you to feel accepted by our family."

"I do. By you, and my siblings and their families, and our cousins."

"You deserve to find love."

"Not disagreeing with you," he said.

"And when you do, I want to meet him. And I want him to feel welcome in my home."

"I'll think about it." He sighed. The ranch's main house was an intrinsic part of Imogen Taylor's life, part of the reason he didn't resent it entirely. But he didn't want to give her false hope. Chances were he wouldn't find a man to love that deeply any time soon. He was so used to drawing thick lines between personal, work and family.

"And now you're holed up in some grimy hotel in a backwater town—"

"I assure you, the sheets are clean," he said dryly.

She sniffed.

"And I do have some semblance of a plan for the evening. I met... Look, there's no need for details." What was the point in letting her think there was something going on with Mike when he didn't even know if he'd get to have another conversation with the guy?

"Oh, I see how it is," she said. "I can't decide whether to tell you to have fun or to remind you to be careful."

"How about I do a little bit of both?"

"All right, dear." Her tone was fond, carrying an *I'm satisfied for now* edge.

After saying goodbye, he put in the precise amount of effort getting ready to look good without it being obvious how much time he'd spent in front of a mirror. Satisfied, he left the inn and strolled the few blocks east.

He headed down the Social Club stairs, heart jogging in time with his steps.

The seat where he'd enjoyed Mike's company yesterday was free. But there wasn't a lanky-framed, smiling man with luxurious brown curls slinging drinks behind the stretch of worn, carved wood.

Resigned, he made his way toward the young woman lining up pint glasses at her workstation. Maybe she knew where Mike was.

The place was fuller than yesterday. Small groups of people clustered around a few of the tables, chatting and enjoying their drinks and pub snacks. An older man sat sentinel at the end of the bar, with a stack of books in front of him—*Quilting for Dummies* stood out. He lifted a steel-gray eyebrow in challenge. Daniel smiled and gave a quick nod. He wasn't about to yuck on someone else's yum.

The bartender's eyes were warm as Daniel approached.

By the way her gaze took in his chest and forearms, he got the impression she appreciated his choice of a plaid Western shirt with the sleeves rolled up. He wasn't going to give her the impression he returned her interest, but he did appreciate the confirmation he looked good, even if he was more casual than usual for a Saturday night.

"Hey there," she said. "What can I get you?"

Well, he's around five-ten and has eyes like the deeper parts of the creek behind my house...

Probably should sound less like an infatuated fourteen-year-old writing terrible poetry about their crush.

"I was hoping Mike was working today," he said.

The woman's hopeful expression dimmed. "Afraid not. He isn't on the schedule until Monday."

"Ah." His heart sank. No doubt the guy was busy on his family's ranch all weekend or hanging out with his nephew. He grimaced. Mike's time off meant there would be a good chance Daniel wouldn't get to see him before his truck was fixed. He couldn't exactly walk around town for two days hoping to cross paths with the guy. There was strategic planning, and then there was stalking. "If you hear from him, feel free to let him know Danny stopped by."

She nodded. "I can pour a beer as well as he can, if you're interested."

He couldn't tell if she was being literal or figurative, so he politely declined.

"If you're needing to fill your Saturday night, the rodeo's in town," she suggested, pointing at a poster stapled to the wall next to a collection of smaller advertisements, ranging from an upcoming glee club event to offers for tutoring to a lost cat.

The text splashed on the colorful rodeo poster detailed the usual events, plus the headlining Hawkins Sisters' barrel-racing performance.

"Appreciate the suggestion," he said, then rapped the bar with his knuckles. He was friends with a number of the Hawkinses, given several of the sisters lived in Bronco, but it had been a while since he'd seen them perform. They never disappointed.

She pursed her lips. "If you *are* looking for Mike, he might be there with Cody. Pretty much everyone I've talked to is going at some point this weekend."

He smiled his appreciation. "Thank you."

It was as good a plan as any. He went to the Tenacity Feed and Seed and picked up a last-minute ticket.

He also called the inn and extended his stay by a couple more nights. Might as well give the mechanic time to fix his truck right.

Or so he'd tell himself to justify trying to meet up with Mike. If he did manage to run into the guy, he'd make sure to get his phone number and to ask him out for coffee or something. Tea, maybe, since Mike had said he preferred it. This whole "chance and circumstance" routine wasn't effective enough, and he didn't like feeling like a borderline creep.

A few hours later, he passed through the entrance to the traveling show, held on the fairgrounds a short walk outside of town. It was a typical open field dotted with clumps of grass and weeds, with the outer plywood sides of the competition ring plastered with logos of local feed stores, farriers and the Tenacity 4-H club. The paint was peeling from the advertisements. They'd probably been up for enough seasons that the people who walked past them didn't even register the faded colors and text anymore. A big stretch of land behind him brimmed with parked trucks and dusty cars, and the area outside of the ring was divided into a rectangle for food trucks and tables and a makeshift stage and picnic table seating. To the side, a small area with games and a bucking bull ride snugged up to one of the ring's walls.

Scents of butter and charcoal smoke mixed with the earthy tang of the animals, throwing Daniel back to going to the rodeo any chance he got when he was a kid. Hell, into his teens and twenties, too, hopped up on sugar and caffeine and the excitement of watching friends and a few of his family members compete in events around Bronco and beyond. Catching the eye of the occasional cute cowboy, too, so long as he knew the guy was interested. In more recent years, any attendance had been more about networking on behalf of Taylor Beef or the Triple T, and he missed the innocent fun of his youth.

A hive of activity buzzed around him. People funneled into the stands surrounding the open air ring, hands laden with hot dogs, cotton candy and popcorn. He'd have to go back later and grab a snack or maybe some ribs. The savory barbecue smells wafting his way promised tangy, saucy goodness.

He made his way to the stands and started climbing. Before he could get more than three rows up, a waving pair of arms flashed in the corner of his vision. He glanced toward the motion and then let out a chuckle. Cody was standing a few rows farther up, doing his best to catch Daniel's attention. A precarious move, considering the kid was holding a hot dog. Mike sat next to the boy, his straw cowboy hat casting a shadow over his eyes. The younger man managed to snatch the half-eaten bun and wiener from his nephew's hand before any condiment-related tragedy could occur. Then he nodded and waved his own hand. Less exuberant than Cody's invitation, but still a clear *come join us*.

The glint of pleasure just visible under the brim of his hat held an even better promise.

Daniel took a deep breath and made his way toward the pair.

"Danny, you're here. I told Grandma and Uncle Mike you'd probably come," the boy crowed.

"I hadn't expected to, but I'm betting it's going to be fun. And thanks for waving me over, Cody."

Before Daniel could put much thought into why he'd been a topic of conversation for the Coopers, Cody scooted closer to Mike, making room for Daniel. Mike didn't correct his nephew.

Using the boy as a buffer? Hmm.

Maybe Mike had wanted to avoid Daniel needing to climb over them both. Or maybe Mike wasn't sure where Daniel preferred to sit and so was giving him an out.

He didn't need one. Nothing sounded better than being elbow-to-elbow, thigh-to-thigh with the younger man.

Chapter Five

Mike stood from his seat in the stands and shook Danny's hand as the Stetson-and-plaid clad man bent to sit next to Cody. Before Danny could settle in on the boy's right, Mike nudged his nephew.

"Scoot over, kiddo. I'll take the middle. I want to give Danny the better view."

I want him next to me, not you.

Cody complied, making room.

Danny put a hand on Mike's hoodie-covered shoulder as he passed by. Their stomachs almost brushed, and Mike caught a subtle trace of cologne. Their gazes collided, Danny's bluer than any man's eyes deserved to be. His dark eyebrow arched and his mouth twitched.

Mike almost groaned. Was the man trying to flirt without being obvious in front of Cody? Or was he giving Mike a silent *I've figured out your ruse* when it came to the seating arrangement?

He didn't seem to mind settling in next to Mike.

His mouth was still curved with the barest fragment of amusement.

Mike would happily kiss that smirk away.

Couldn't, though—not in the middle of half the town, with his nephew by his side. Something new like this needed to be tested, tried on in private.

Swallowing his frustration, he sat again. Danny's strong, cotton-covered biceps pressed into Mike's. *Mmm.* The hoodie Mike had on over his T-shirt didn't mute the excitement at all. No layers of clothing could dull the pleasure of brushing against the other man.

Danny's shirt wasn't anything different than Mike might wear on a weekend, but skimming those chest muscles, it looked like something you'd see on a Times Square billboard.

"I didn't expect you to still be here," Mike said. "Your truck's still in the shop?"

"You know how car repairs go." Danny's cheeks turned a faint pink. "Don't want to overstay my welcome, but…"

Mike nudged him with an elbow. "No complaints from me."

The color on his new friend's face deepened. "I'm hoping to make the best of my time in Tenacity. The rodeo seemed like a good place to start on a Saturday night."

"Not many other choices around here," Mike said, his curiosity growing. *Make the best of my time* could mean so many things. And damn, he wanted to know if he factored into Danny's plans.

When the other man didn't reply right away, Mike said, "The crowd at the Social Club will be small tonight."

"I dropped in for a few minutes this afternoon," Danny said, running a hand down his face as if he was hiding a bit of embarrassment.

Looking for me?

Satisfied warmth heated Mike's belly. "The sunshine made you thirsty?"

"Something like that." Danny leaned sideways, enough to bump shoulders for a second. "Went there to look for you, but found you here instead. Your coworker said you might have tickets tonight. I came for the sake of the show, but I'm not sad I ran into you."

"A fortunate accident." Mike felt like his smile was as out of control as the riot in his chest.

"Who had an accident?" Cody piped up.

Danny chuckled.

"No one, Code." Mike ruffled his nephew's hair and passed him a napkin from his pocket to deal with the ketchup on his face.

The boy's brows knitted together, and then he shrugged and took another big bite, not bothering to finish swallowing before he peered around Mike to ask, "Do you like barrel racing or bronc riding best?"

"Oof, tough choice," Danny said, his expression thoughtful. "Might depend on the competition. But I'm thinking tonight it's going to be the barrel racing. The Hawkins Sisters always put on a good show. I wonder which sisters will be performing."

"Not Amy—she's pregnant," Mike said. "Getting married this month."

"You bartenders, knowing all the gossip."

Mike laughed. "Yeah, her fiancé, Josh, came in for some advice a few weeks ago. I'm glad the two of them figured things out."

Danny nodded. "The Hawkins family is as hard to keep track of as mine is."

Cody's eyes blinked wide. "You know them?"

The handsome cowboy paused long enough to suggest he was scrambling for an answer. "My mom knows their grandmother well. And I run into them in—at home sometimes."

"Oh, *wow*." The eight-year-old amazement knew no bounds. "Could we go meet them?"

Danny looked almost nervous but then erased it with an easy smile. "Probably not at the last minute. They're busy, getting ready to perform and then packing up."

Mike appreciated the kind refusal. Danny might not have

known much about kids, but he knew enough not to make promises he couldn't uphold.

Taking the denial in stride, Cody pelted them both with enough questions about the rodeo and the specific events to fill the overflowing bookcase in his room twice over.

Mike scrubbed a hand over his nephew's head. "One of these days you're going to start writing down all the things you're learning, and you'll end up with an encyclopedia."

"What's an encyclopedia?" Cody asked.

"It's like an online database for storing all sorts of information about things," Mike answered. "Kind of like a dictionary for facts."

Danny guffawed and nudged Mike with an elbow. "Or, you know, a set of books sitting on your grandparents' bookcase. One you combed through whenever you were home sick from school and bored because they didn't have cable." Humor danced in his eyes. "No? Just me?"

"Yeah, just you," Mike replied, matching the teasing gaze. "But Cody *does* love learning about dinosaurs."

Jaw dropping, Danny held a palm to his chest. *"Ouch."*

Regret coursed through Mike. *Too far.*

"Damn, sorry," he mumbled.

"I can take it," Danny said, touching Mike's knee, letting his fingers linger for a few seconds. "I'm well aware I'm older than you."

"I don't mind," Mike said, pitching his voice low in hopes Cody would miss the subtle message.

Danny paused, studying Mike with an intense look. It might have made Mike uncomfortable were he not deeply, deeply hoping that intensity would translate to something more.

A small hand tugged on Mike's sleeve.

"Uncle Mike! The *anthem*."

Yanking off his hat, Mike shot to his feet, Danny close behind. Heat washed up his face at how damn enchanted he'd been by those dark brown eyes, so much so he'd lost track of both his nephew's attention and the assortment of flags and horses.

When the anthem ended, Danny put his own hat back on but stayed standing. "I should get a drink. Can I get you something? Cody, too? Whatever you want. The lemonade looked freshly squeezed."

"It is. Town specialty. But you don't have to treat us." Between the guy's repair bill and the nightly charges at the inn, his wallet had to be emptying out fast.

Danny waved off Mike's refusal. "Happy to."

"Lemonades, then. Thank you."

Damn, Danny had taken off quickly. *Had* Mike hurt the older man's feelings with his careless joke?

He shook out his hair and then ran a hand through it before fixing his hat back in place. He was *not* good at this. Likely why he'd been so unlucky in love, or even in lust, so far. Inept and awkward and destined to turn off any man who was remotely interesting.

He sighed and tried to enjoy the spectacle in front of him.

The whirl of activity in the ring held Cody in thrall. A high-school stunt racer, warming up the crowd, was taking her horse through its paces.

Taking advantage of his nephew's rapt attention elsewhere, Mike checked his texts.

He flicked from his mom's don't forget I have quilting club Monday evening to Jenna's running late—Robbie's fussy—might not make it.

Prior to Danny showing up, he would have been disappointed to find out his best friend was threatening to be a no-show. Now it seemed like a golden opportunity to hang out with the out-of-towner without an audience.

Well, an audience except for Cody, but his nephew didn't seem to be tuned into Mike's interest in Danny.

Mike pointed at the turquoise-spangled stunt rider. "She's good, eh?"

His nephew's eyes were as wide as the barrel tops.

When the competitor finished an awe-inspiring shoulder stand, Cody let out a "Holy *crap*," then slapped a hand over his mouth.

"I know. It's amazing what a human and a horse can do when they're a team."

"Danny missed it," Cody said, face falling.

"There will be more. And it sounds like he's watched a few rodeos. Look." Mike pointed to the bottom of the grandstand. "There he is."

Danny carried a paper carton tray of three lemonades and a sleeve of popcorn. He looked a little sheepish as he scooted past Mike again and took his seat. He handed out the drinks and then passed over the popcorn.

"This okay for Cody?"

Mike nodded.

"Awesome—thanks!" Cody exclaimed.

"You're welcome." Danny rubbed the back of his neck and sent Mike a look of apology. "I couldn't resist."

"It's Cody's favorite," Mike said. "Part of a special night out, too. I was going to get him some a little later."

Between the popcorn and the announcement of the next competitor, Cody was lost to the experience, his attention rapt.

Mike always enjoyed watching the performances, but he was more interested in the man next to him. Danny's arrival in town was the best surprise, and sharing a bench with him was even more welcome.

"Did you hoof it out here?"

"Yeah. Way shorter walk than I did from the highway yesterday," Danny replied with a laugh.

"No need to walk back to town when you're done. I could drop you back at the inn…unless you have something arranged."

"I'd appreciate it. I'm not used to relying on people's generosity like this."

It made Mike wonder if his new friend wasn't often in situations where other people were taking control.

"This company you work for," Mike started, then frowned. Danny had given him so little detail on what he actually did. "Where is it?"

"Around Bronco," Danny said cautiously.

"What do you do for them?"

The crowd roared as the current rider managed to stand at a right angle to the ground.

Danny whistled and didn't reply.

"I'm starting to think you're CIA or something."

His chuckle erupted to a laugh. "Nothing nearly so interesting. HR management, for the most part. I enjoy it, but it's boring as hell to explain." He cleared his throat. "Do you like working for your family? Are you a partner, or are your parents in charge?"

Mike shrugged. "My dad and I share the load, for the most part. My mom used to take more of an active role, but she's had to up her nursing hours as the beef market's tightened."

Danny's mouth flattened. "I hear you. Is that why you bartend?"

"Yup."

"Tenacity seems like the kind of place where everyone helps each other out."

"It is. We've had to be. Used to have more money flowing through Tenacity, until the Deroy family left town with a chunk of the town savings. Or at least, we all believed they were at fault."

Danny's dark brows rose toward the underside of his pristine black Stetson. "Sounds like there's a story there."

"Mmm." Mike glanced at Cody, who was cramming a giant handful of popcorn into his mouth. Kernels spilled out the

sides of his grip, raining onto the floor. He was well fascinated by the show, still, so Mike had at least a few minutes
to talk shop.

"They were a family who used to hold a lot of sway around
here. Disappeared about fifteen years ago. A fortune disappeared from the town coffers around the same time, and we
all assumed it was connected to the Deroys. Their name has
been mud since."

Danny winced. "I take it the town hasn't recovered from
the loss?"

"No. There was talk about a town-revitalization project
back then, but when the money disappeared, the group backed
out. And then one by one, some of the businesses in town
folded. Not all of them, obviously, but enough that we've been
scrambling ever since. I mean, the town struggles have been
all I've ever known—I was barely a teenager when the Deroys left—but it's hard to see the place I love never seem to
get ahead. The *people* I love." Mike sighed. He sounded bitter, but then, he *was*. Knowing his mom had to commute to a
job she no longer wanted because they needed her income to
pay the bills stung his heart and his pride, even though he was
doing what he could. "Tenacity is home, but the economy's
tough. It's hard for local ranchers to make ends meet, and the
duplicity made things worse. And now we don't even know
if it was the Deroys who took the money."

"Got a mystery on your hands?"

"Sure do. Last month, my friend Nina Sanchez and her
great uncle found a huge stash of money hidden on a piece of
property the mayor used to own. Seems like the money never
left town after all."

Danny's jaw dropped. Unlike Cody, he was ignoring the
show. "No way."

Mike nodded. "Had a note with it and everything. 'You
got the wrong man.'"

"Who wrote it?"

Lifting a shoulder, Mike said, "No one knows. And no one's sure who hid the money, either. Barrett Deroy, maybe. Or the mayor, or even someone else." He shook his head. "It's a damned mess. I even heard a rumor the Deroys might even be returning to town."

"Must be the talk of the Social Club."

"Sure is. I end up hearing a different angle each shift I work."

"Quite the story." Danny frowned. "Are your local ranchers connecting with the state livestock organization? Getting the support they need?"

It took effort to hold in his scoff. "We've tried. Not much they can do about the prices we get from the feed lots given how much of it is controlled by the meatpackers. I know they're lobbying the powers that be, but it'll still be too late for some of my neighbors." He scrubbed his hands down his face. "Between the town finances and the damn real-estate vultures swooping around Cooper Ranch, I can't say I'm one to trust the wealthy cattlemen who run the livestock organization."

Danny's ensuing sigh was more like a hiss. "Sorry to hear it's been a rough go."

"I've seen too many people taken under by greed," he said quietly.

One by one, his neighbors had fallen to a lack of profits or legal challenges. Seeing people selling off their herds when they couldn't get a fair price at auction to keep their ranches running broke his heart. Even worse had been when a large seed company had targeted one of the Coopers' neighbors with a BS lawsuit. Mike would always be infuriated they'd come after a hardworking farmer trying to survive, just because a few seeds had spread in the wind and ended up in their field.

"It's terrifying in some cases," he continued. "I keep waiting for someone to come after us next or that we'll have a year where we're too in the red and Dad will have to sell off more of the herd than he already has."

Mike had only seen Larry Cooper cry once—while watching trailers cart away half of the animals he'd sweated and bled for. Mike would not let that happen again.

"Damn. Scary stuff," Danny said, shifting awkwardly.

"Scary, and super depressing. Sorry. I didn't mean to go off on a big tangent about money."

"It's okay. I just… I can't imagine money corrupts everyone who has it, yeah? Someone's moral code isn't always connected to their wallet." He was biting the inside of his lip.

Mike shrugged. "Maybe not, but I've never had a rich guy prove me wrong."

Hell, one of the men who'd come to town to try to convince Mike's parents to sell their spread last summer had even pretended to fall for Mike to gain an advantage with the Coopers.

Mike's first few romantic failures had been amateur hour compared to the crowning embarrassment of being taken in by Steven's duplicity.

Not a story he planned to share with Danny, especially not in front of Cody.

Mike nudged his nephew with an elbow, startling the boy, who was fascinated by a goofy rodeo clown's antics. At some point during his story, the trick riders had finished, and they were setting up for the next event.

Danny leaned forward to catch Cody's attention. "Who's been your favorite so far?"

Cody answered with his usual torrent of happiness, oblivious to how serious Mike and Danny's discussion had gotten. Mike could tell, though—he'd annihilated the mood.

"Hey," he said, clapping his hands together. "How about we go get funnel cakes? My treat."

"Really? Uncle Mike, it *is* the best night ever," Cody said gleefully.

Mike forced a smile. "I hope so, bud."

He'd been a buzzkill, but maybe dessert could turn things around.

Chapter Six

Daniel accepted a paper plate overflowing with a funnel cake from Mike. His head was still spinning after the conversation about Tenacity.

He'd learned a slew of interesting facts about the town, most of which made his heart ache for the hardworking ranchers in the area.

More importantly, Mike had revealed a hell of a lot about himself, and Daniel was left reeling.

Mike wasn't like some of the people Daniel had dated, who'd waited until dinner was half over to announce they'd forgotten their credit card, blinking at him innocently until he offered to pay for the meal. Hell, in all those situations he'd have offered to pay anyway, but being treated like an ATM always soured his stomach. Worse was the number of times he'd been asked if Taylors had to sign prenups or what exact share he owned in the Triple T. He hadn't gotten a similar vibe from Mike at all, but he'd been happy to let the theory go untested for a few days.

Turned out he'd been worried about the exact wrong thing. Daniel's money wouldn't attract Mike—it would repel him. Had Daniel been open about being a Taylor from the moment he'd sat down at the bar, he doubted the younger man would have welcomed any flirting at all. No way would they be standing a few inches from each other, watching Cody chow down on a deep-fried treat.

And why shouldn't Mike be cautious? From the sounds of it, anyone who'd come through Tenacity with money before had left a trail of damage behind them. Daniel wasn't naive—he saw the ways greed poisoned people. He'd always aimed not to be like that. But he suspected Mike was going to have a hard time seeing the difference.

Hell. What was the best way to handle it? Hiding his last name forever would be both impossible and dishonest, but he needed more time with Mike without having his bank account getting in the way. He couldn't risk the younger man jumping to conclusions about who Daniel was and what he wanted based on the state of his investment portfolio. Taylor Beef did hold a lot of sway and influence in the market, but they weren't involved in predatory lawsuits with farmers, nor were they coming after smaller producers with dishonest, unfair property bids.

They were a big business, but at the root of it was still a family business. It fed into Daniel's reasons for the decades he'd spent trying to change his father's and uncles' backward views rather than walking away—his generation, he and his siblings and cousins, were going to breathe new life into Taylor Beef over time. The shift was often slow, but it was possible.

Something he'd *like* to talk about with Mike.

He didn't know what to do. If he didn't find a good time to be honest and Mike found out he was a Taylor, it could be unforgivable.

The last thing he wanted to do was appear like one more lying rich dude.

"You don't like your funnel cake, Danny?" Cody asked. Daniel didn't need to ask if the boy liked his own dessert—half of the powdered sugar was decorating his mouth and cheeks.

Daniel shook himself out of his thoughts. "I'm so excited to eat it, it made me nervous to start."

Mike, who'd been tearing off parts of the nest of dough into careful bites, grinned. "Cody's not much for anticipation. He's more of a dive-right-in kind of guy."

Daniel smiled. "I can appreciate that. My brother Ryan likes to approach the world head first. I've learned to be cautious, though. And to savor the excitement when something truly epic comes along."

"I can go either way," Mike said. "Depends on the day and what there is to get excited about."

"Funnel cakes don't make the 'dive right in' list?" Daniel asked, giving Mike's tidy handling of his dessert a meaningful glance.

Mike's gaze glinted a deep whiskey gold, the green lost to the setting sun. "I keep getting distracted by other, more interesting options."

"There is a lot to look at," Daniel teased, giving the other man a look of his own.

He glanced around the choices for food or family entertainment, set up in a large, makeshift courtyard of sorts. With the dimming natural light, the strands of lights framing the food booths showed up more, an array of mismatched colors. Farther into the sectioned-off area, plywood boards displayed tacked-up prizes for the kids who conquered the midway games. Every second person who passed nodded or waved at Mike or called out a hello. Mike returned each greeting in kind.

"I love nights like this. Anticipation is my catnip," Mike said. He wasn't paying any attention to the giant Plinko board, the row of Skee-Ball stations or the basketball shooting game with prizes on display, row upon row of stuffed animals tacked to a plywood sheet. His eyes were fixed to Daniel's face. "And when it comes to spontaneity, I can go either way depending on the circumstance. But this weekend, I'm feeling like life wants me to say yes."

"Yes to what?" Daniel murmured. He was dying to know what the younger man was anticipating.

"That's the question, isn't it?"

Daniel couldn't quite read the vague answer, but if he had his way, Mike would be saying yes to getting to know each other better. A bit of time alone, even.

The tension snapped when Cody held out his empty plate. He gazed at Daniel's untouched funnel cake with a tinge of envy.

Mike ruffled his nephew's hair. "No mooching. I bought it for Danny, not so you could have seconds. But how about we go test my arm at the baseball-pitching game? It's been a while since high-school gym class, but I bet I could hit enough targets to win you something."

There was something so damn wholesome about watching the interplay between a caring adult and a well-loved child. Daniel could remember having similar moments with his mom but not so much with his dad or uncles. They staunchly believed in showing love by building Taylor Beef. Passing on the love of the land, of hard work, of tradition. Not by sharing carnival-style treats and trying to win stuffed animals.

He was liking the Cooper tradition better.

"Mike! There you are!"

A fair-skinned woman around Mike's age scooted her way through the crowd. The baby carrier strapped to her chest covered most of the top of the flowered dress she'd paired with some decorative leather boots. A stern-faced baby faced out from the carrier, staring intently at the crowd around her. Had to be the woman's child, given their identical red hair color. A tiny, chubby fist gripped the end of the woman's braid.

Mike turned toward the voice, then held his arms open. "Jenna, you made it."

"We did. Someone calmed down enough." She hugged him, making a gentle baby sandwich.

"Jenna, can I see Robbie?" Cody interrupted, standing on his toes.

"As long as she stays in the carrier, honey. She's too fussy to come out to say hi."

Cody got up close and offered the baby a sticky finger and some peekaboo faces.

The boy's ease with the baby made Daniel smile.

Jenna's gaze landed on Daniel. Her eyes widened before flicking to Mike. "Michael Cooper, are you on a *date*?"

Mike winced. "More like ran into a friend, Jenna." He wiped a hand down his face. "This is Danny. He's from out of town. Danny, my best friend, Jenna Lattimore."

"No wonder you weren't fussed about me arriving late." She stuck out her hand for Danny to shake. Her firm grip carried a hitch of a warning, and she gave him an up-and-down so quick he would have missed it were he not used to making split-second assessments of people at work. "I haven't heard a word about you, Danny, which means Mike actually likes you, and *that* means I should go somewhere else."

"Jenna." Mike's lifted brow screamed *tone it down*.

She blinked innocently at her friend.

"Did Diego come?" Mike asked, before glancing at Daniel and adding, "Jenna's fiancé."

"He's in line for ribs. Helping out Noah Trent with his boys, I think." Jenna rubbed the baby's tummy through the carrier. "My goodness, that man has his hands full with three toddlers who love to run and only two hands to catch them. I mean, I know he has his parents to help, but still."

Mike winced. "Yeah, I saw Noah earlier. He hasn't stopped by the Social Club much lately—understandable—and man, it looks like he hasn't slept in months. Made me thankful this guy has no problem clocking ten hours every night."

He ruffled his nephew's hair.

Daniel held in a wince of his own. He didn't have a clue

who Jenna and Mike were talking about, but he'd seen Eloise and her husband, Diego, chasing after Merry, and even one toddler looked like a handful.

Jenna tsked. "Look at us, getting sidetracked around your company. Sorry, Danny, I didn't mean to hijack your evening with Tenacity scuttlebutt you have no context for."

"All good," he assured her. "You can join us, if you like."

He didn't want Mike to feel pressured to ditch his plans with his friends just because Daniel had showed up unexpectedly.

"Oh, no no no. Robbie and I are going to get out of your hair and join Diego."

"Okay, then," Daniel said.

"Mmm, yes. I hope you have a *more*-than-okay time," she said with a smile before dropping a noisy kiss on Cody's forehead and sidling away. "I'll text you, Mike."

"Nice to meet you," Daniel called after her, suppressing a laugh.

"I am so sorry," Mike said, his hazel gaze shuttering.

"I'm not." He'd somehow managed to pass the preliminary best-friend test. "I'm sorry I got in the way of your plans to meet up with her."

"You didn't," Mike insisted. "And as you can see, she was all about leaving me in your capable hands."

"Happy to qualify as capable," he murmured.

Mike's cheeks turned sunburn pink.

"Uncle Mike!" Cody seemed oblivious to the adult conversation. "Can we play some games?"

"If Danny's up for it."

"Of course," Daniel said.

Mike led them over to the booth and handed over a twenty and got an apple basket heaped with softballs. Black-and-gray marks and scratches flecked the white surfaces, and more than one had loose stitching. The booth had various targets, both vertical bull's-eyes as well as metal milk jugs and apple crates.

Cody emptied half the basket trying to hit the bull's-eyes. Mike coached him calmly, helping Cody fix his form until he hit three targets.

The attendant waved a hand at the smallest prizes, a row of garish purple-and-orange stuffed lizards. "Pick one."

Cody looked up at Mike. "We can't win a big one?"

"Not enough baseballs, kiddo," Mike answered. "We're down to four left."

The girl running the booth couldn't have been more than seventeen. Her blond hair was in a high ponytail, and she was chewing a wad of gum rivaling the size of one of the baseballs. Her expression was beyond bored as she pointed to the assortment of targets. "If you hit all the bull's-eyes and land a ball in each jug and basket with no misses, you get your choice of prizes."

"The *big prizes*?" Cody yelped.

"Yeah, that's what I said," the teen replied with an eye roll. "You need ten balls to do it."

It threw Daniel back to when his sister Charlotte had been in high school and had been equal parts skeptical and sass.

Cody was too enraptured by the sight of the three-foot-tall stuffed animals hanging from the top of the prize board to care about the attitude. "Uncle Mike, you need to win me one. *Pleeeeease.*"

"How much for six balls?" Daniel asked the girl.

"Ten bucks," she said.

Daniel pulled out his wallet and handed over a bill.

"I don't think my aim's good enough to do it with no misses," Mike said. "Put a rope in my hand and I can hook a hundred pairs of horns, but I think I'd miss at least one if I tried to get all the targets and jugs."

Daniel cocked a brow at the visual. "I would love to see that."

"Me missing targets?"

"No, you roping steers."

"The competitors in the event later will be more impressive than I would," Mike said.

Daniel shook his head. "I doubt it."

It earned him twin patches of red on Mike's cheeks.

"*You'd* look good doing pretty much anything." The whispered compliment landed with a wallop. It was Daniel's turn to blush.

"Yeah? Well, how about I put your theory to the test and win your nephew a giant SpongeBob?"

Cody looked up with solemn eyes. "Could I pick which prize I want?"

"Of course. *If* I win." He smiled at the kid. "I'll do my best. Though I haven't played since college."

"Like, rec-league playing? Or better?" Mike asked, an interested glint lighting his eyes.

"A few levels above rec league." He might've had his name engraved on a trophy or two.

"How far up?"

"Uh, NCAA national finalists?"

Mike's jaw dropped.

Daniel's gut urged him to minimize. "D2, not D1. And it's been a long time."

"So modest."

He lifted a shoulder. "No use bragging. Not like I played pro or anything."

It had been so much easier to fly under the radar.

"Well, time to show off, all-star," Mike said.

He exhaled and tossed the ball from hand to hand. "Phew. *Bases loaded, bottom of the ninth* has got nothing on this."

Figuring the bull's-eye targets were the easiest and would give him the chance to warm up, he started on those, knocking all four off one after the other. Each time, Cody cheered.

Daniel eyed the row of milk jugs. The rims were subtly

bent, so a ball would careen off if it landed wrong and spun around.

Mike stood right next to him. His arms were crossed, but he was close enough to stretch out a couple of his fingers and run his fingertips right above Daniel's left elbow, an electric touch through the long sleeve of his shirt. "Second thoughts about making promises?"

He shook his head. "Just calculating."

Cody crossed his arms, mimicking his uncle. "Keep your eyes on where you're throwing, not on the ball," he said solemnly, passing on the advice he'd received himself a few minutes ago.

"Solid tip. Thank you," Daniel said, lobbing a ball underhand in hopes it swooped right through the jug opening, without spiraling and bouncing out. It landed in the bottom of the jug with a satisfying clunk.

He followed it up with two more and then one of the sideways apple baskets, nailed to the backboard. Arguably the toughest—if he bounced it off the back at all, it would pop right out.

Mike whistled. "You are good."

Cody was bouncing on his toes. "Oh, *wow*, Danny."

"Don't count your chickens quite yet, okay?"

Fat chance. Visions of life-size animal stuffies were dancing in the kid's eyes.

Mike went to step away.

Daniel caught him and pulled him back. "Stay there. You're committed to being my good-luck charm."

Mike's mouth crept into a half smile. He brushed Daniel's arm with his fingertips again.

Heart skipping a beat, Daniel controlled his breathing and lobbed two more balls into the horizontal baskets.

The attendant was watching with wide eyes now, no longer bored by her task.

Mike leaned into Daniel's ear. His breath teased the lobe and tickled the hair at his temple. "One more to go. What prize do *you* want if you win?"

He shivered. "Take me for a ride."

A choking sound filled his ear, and Mike's fingers tightened around his arm.

Daniel's stomach sank as the unintended double entendre hit him. "I mean, on a horse, on your ranch. Not—damn it, I didn't mean to suggest…"

He tossed the ball. It bounced out of the basket and fell to the ground.

He groaned.

Cody yelped in disappointment. He looked up at Daniel and Mike, lower lip wobbling.

Mike let go of Daniel and palmed the top of his hat. "My bad, Code. I threw Danny off his game."

The teen sent Cody a sympathetic look. "Nine balls almost count as a win. You could trade the small one in for a medium-size one."

"So I could have the allosaurus?" Cody asked in a small voice.

"What, the T. rex?" she said.

"It's an allosaurus. It has three front claws on each arm, not two."

The girl laughed. "Sure, kid. Consider it yours."

Cody took the stuffy with reverent hands, though he passed it off to Mike a minute later when he spotted a massive bouncy slide and begged to be able to go on it.

Five minutes later, Daniel was alone with Mike. They stood to the side, behind a group of chattering parents.

"What about my prize?" Daniel asked. "Do I get to trade up for getting nine of ten targets?"

Mike's gaze flashed. The back of his hand brushed Daniel's. "What, you still want to come to the ranch? Take a tour on horseback, maybe without Cody?"

Before Daniel could talk himself out of it, he threaded his fingers into the warm, waiting hand and tugged. Mike spun toward him until their chests were an inch apart.

Their lips, too. He caught the scent of powdered sugar and chocolate. Would Mike taste sweet?

He leaned in.

Mike met him halfway. A brush, a second or two of contact.

Enough to register a hint of a taste. Not traces of sugar.

Just…addictive.

He cupped the back of Mike's head, right below his hat, and stole another peck before standing back.

"Yeah, I still want to come to your ranch." In fact, it would be the perfect time to work in his last name. "Invitation good for tomorrow?"

"Sure, Danny." A mischievous look crossed the other man's face. "I'm all yours."

Chapter Seven

Sunday morning, Daniel lounged in the small guest area of the inn, waiting for Mike to arrive while trying not to seem overeager. It was all he could do not to pace, though. After their brief kisses last evening, the rest of the rodeo had been focused on Cody and on enjoying the show. The boy had recounted the highlights for the whole ride from the fairgrounds to dropping Daniel at the inn. A fun time, for sure, but after the slivers of flirtation he'd traded with Mike whenever Cody's head had been turned, he was looking forward to the possibility of more. Even if it was only a conversation and another kiss.

Emphasis on the conversation. Mike was welcoming him into his home today, onto the ranch that meant so much to the Cooper family. Daniel needed to be upfront about his own family as soon as he could. Mike was either going to be good with the truth or he wouldn't.

If it was the second, Daniel might find himself with a long walk back to downtown Tenacity.

Thankfully Mike had promised they'd be alone.

Daniel's excitement had foiled his attempt to sleep in. He wished he could have, for the sake of wanting the wait to pass quicker. But he'd been up with the birds nesting in the tree outside his window.

This whole *hang around town in hopes of romancing a*

man, but be elusive enough as not to be clingy routine was
not for the impatient.

He couldn't remember the last time he'd pulled up a chair
and spent a morning reading a novel. His perch in the lounge
gave him a view of the parking lot through one of the wide
windows.

A black truck pulled in at twelve on the nose.

Damn, punctuality was sexy.

Daniel had a post-ride change of clothes in a backpack in
case he got dusty. He stuck his novel alongside his spare outfit,
fixed his black Stetson on his head and headed for the front
door, trying to look casual.

He did not feel casual. Not at all. His insides crackled and
sparked like a chain of firecrackers.

"Have fun out at the Coopers' place, honey! Say hello to
that godson of mine for me," Carol called from behind the
front desk. She was standing with a white woman who was
probably a little younger than Daniel, whose brown hair was
pulled into a ponytail. The curiosity in her gaze matched
Carol's.

"Mmm, yes, have fun," the younger woman called. "Say
hi for me—Chrissy—too."

He nodded and put two fingers to the brim of his hat in a
brief tip. "Will do. Nice to meet you, Chrissy. Have a good afternoon."

Cheeks heating over his business being public knowledge—
or at least Mike's family having an inkling of what was going
on—he ducked out into the midday sun.

Mike had pulled under the portico. The driver's door swung
open, but Daniel strode over and got into the passenger seat
before his ride could get out.

"In a hurry?" Mike asked. Amusement tugged at his mouth.
His hair was a perfect mess of sun-kissed brown waves and,
without a hat covering it, was begging for fingers to dig into

it. He wore faded, fitted jeans and a plain black T-shirt high-lighting every ounce of muscle the man had earned out on his ranch.

Daniel swallowed, trying to get moisture back in his mouth. Damn, a person didn't deserve to look so edible.

Hopefully Daniel's own choice of jeans and a navy snap-front work shirt was casual enough. He knew his boots, the ones he'd worn to the rodeo last night, still held the shine of being on the dressier side. He'd packed them to wear while in real-estate meetings in North Dakota. They were quality enough to hold up to a long ride, but if they needed a deep clean after today, so be it.

"I'm excited," he admitted. "My life's been too much work, no play as of late."

Mike paused with his hand on the door handle. "Me, too."

"The excitement, or too much working?"

"Both. I always like playing tour guide. Tenacity might be small, but my heart is here. On the ranch, specifically."

For a moment, Daniel wished he could stay in this small town forever. For all its disadvantages, right now Tenacity seemed like a piece of paradise. But no vista could compare to messy curls and a mouth that could do no wrong.

Smiling, kissing, talking.

All of the above. Daniel was not picky when it came to Mike Cooper.

"I'd kiss you," Mike said, "but Aunt Carol and Chrissy Hastings Parker keep glancing out the doors at us, and I'm not much for being the topic of conversation of all the folks who head to the diner for lunch after church."

"I've never been someone's secret before," Daniel mused. "They both say hello, by the way."

"You're not a secret," Mike said, starting the truck and then leaving the parking lot. "I just don't like speculation around my relationships."

"Talking from experience?"

Mike grimaced and slowed for a four-way stop along the main street. "Yeah. Uh... I've had a couple of less-than-ideal breakups. My last one, in particular."

"Nothing like a broken romance to get a small-town diner buzzing," Daniel said. "Not much different where I come from. Was your ex local?"

"No," Mike said.

Daniel waited, but no elaboration followed. He frowned. "The gossip must have been invasive."

"Under the guise of concern. Full of sympathy and offers of help. And I was..."

Embarrassed? Hurt? Heartbroken? Daniel could make some guesses but didn't want to say the wrong thing.

Mike sighed. "I was left looking like a fool for having trusted a liar."

Well, damn. Made it all the more important for him to be upfront.

What on earth had made him think he'd be starting a relationship off right by hiding something so key to who he was, even if it only lasted a few days? That wasn't the kind of man he aimed to be. He prided himself on being honest with people, and he despised the idea of giving Mike evidence to the contrary.

He'd tell Mike today. Today for sure. At a moment where it wasn't going to seem like he was comparing himself to the people who'd done Mike wrong in his life.

"Sorry you were treated so poorly," Daniel said. Surmising that Mike didn't want to talk more about his breakup, he said, "But we don't have to dwell on it, unless you want to."

"There is nothing I want to talk about less, Danny," Mike said, dry humor twitching at the corners of his mouth.

"Fair, fair. Uh, how long has the ranch been in your family?"

Mike's tense shoulders relaxed, and he latched on to the question. They chatted about ranching on the way out of town.

Soon enough, they were headed onto Cooper land, between two fields and toward a collection of buildings off in the distance. It was one of those clear spring days where Montana earned its Big Sky moniker. Pale fields stretched out under a bluebird sky, far enough to make it hard to believe there were mountains miles beyond the horizon. It was a stunning piece of property and not hard to connect the beauty of it to the proud smile creeping up to crinkle the corners of Mike's eyes.

A fraction of the size of the Taylor holdings, but then, most ranches were.

Despite Mike having hinted at the challenges of the current economy for his parents, the fencing was pristine and the horses grazing in the field to the left were gorgeous animals. As Mike slowed the truck to go over a cattle guard and then to tuck in next to the largest barn, Daniel caught a bit of wear on some of the outbuildings and what he assumed was the main farmhouse, but nothing he'd categorize as neglect, like he'd seen in other areas of Tenacity. Then again, Mike had mentioned the Coopers had sold off some of their herd, so they clearly hadn't escaped having to make hard choices and sacrifices as the town had struggled.

"Home sweet home." Mike swept a hand to encompass the two-story dwelling, the barns and a paddock to their right. "Well, my parents' home anyway. Mine is down the side driveway and behind the tree line over there."

"Not much different from the set up I had on my family's spread, before I moved into town last year."

"Oh, yeah? Why'd you move?"

Oof, how to explain it? After the Thanksgiving blow-up with his dad, he'd needed distance. He'd bought a place in Bronco Heights. Necessary space. The emotional freedom of no longer living within spitting distance of his dad's outdated perspectives balanced out the isolation that came from rattling around alone in his spacious house.

"My dad's not easy to deal with," he settled on. "And living on the ranch meant tolerating an unacceptable level of BS."

Mike whistled. "Damn, life can be complicated sometimes."

"Truth." Crossing his fingers the other man didn't ask for details, Danny asked, "Are we going to ride out from your place or from here?"

"From here. I thought we could take a picnic with us. There's a creek about an hour's ride away."

For a casual Sunday afternoon with a guy who was passing through town, Mike had put a lot of effort into this. Daniel couldn't stop the smile that the extra care brought to his face. It probably bordered on smitten, but it was impossible to hide just how sweet he found Mike's thoughtfulness.

The special treatment made him even angrier that some reprobate had come to town and tried to take advantage of Mike's good-hearted nature.

"You went all out," he said.

Mike paled. "Sorry. Is it too much?"

"No, it's—"

Those hazel eyes squeezed shut. "I always go overboard."

"Stop." He put his hand on Mike's shoulder. The other man opened his eyes slowly, warily. "I think it's great. No one's taken the time to spoil me in a while. Thank you."

"Well, don't get too excited yet." Mike put his hand over Daniel's, stroking his fingers with a warm, work-roughened thumb. "It's just sandwiches, a few hours on a horse and some conversation."

Daniel didn't want to be too obvious, but there was nothing else he wanted to be doing at the moment. He squeezed Mike's shoulder before sliding his hand away.

"Come on inside," Mike said. "No risk of running into my parents—they're off running errands with Cody."

Following his host out of the truck and across the stretch of asphalt to the front porch, Daniel had to beat back surprise. He didn't mind the idea of meeting Mike's parents at all. Not in the sense of *Mom, Dad, here's the guy I'm dating*, because that seemed like getting ahead of himself, but the sheer curiosity of discovering whether Mike's kindness and easygoing demeanor was nature, nurture or from somewhere else entirely. He fascinated Daniel, and so did his roots.

They entered the kitchen of the farmhouse, a bright and cheery room with white walls and gingham-print curtains on the windows. The person in charge of decorating loved themselves a knickknack and had leaned into a cow motif. A row of china animals in a range of styles and sizes peered at the room from the window ledge over the wide sink. Cow puns covered the tea towels hanging from the oven handle. And even though most of the glass-doored hutch stretched along one wall was full of classic white dinnerware, it also held milk jugs, a sugar bowl and salt-and-pepper shakers shaped in silly bovine forms. Daniel smiled. After growing up with his mom being ultraconscious of her role in Bronco society, he appreciated a household that didn't take life seriously all the time.

He took a deep whiff of the air, catching garlic and rosemary. Whatever was in the Crock-Pot on the counter promised a full belly of well-seasoned food.

"I'd give you the tour, but I'm thinking the grounds are more interesting than the house. Besides, it's not really my space anymore, you know? Other than the kitchen. Cody and I eat here a lot. He has a bedroom upstairs, too," Mike said as he made his way to the fridge and pulled out two large metal water bottles and some plastic containers, which he slotted into an insulated bag from under the counter.

"Sounds like your family does ranch living right. The closeness, the camaraderie."

Mike winced. "Yeah, I'm sorry you don't have that, given

what you said about your dad. But what about the rest of your family?"

"Closeness hasn't been our forte," he said carefully. "Other than working with my brothers, Seth and Ryan, my siblings and I were distant in our teens and twenties. There are twelve years between us all—I'm oldest, and Eloise is youngest—but also, it took a while to get past how we were raised. My sisters went their separate ways for a while. I've spent the past couple years getting to know them as adults. With them starting to partner up, and Ryan, too, plus a couple of kids and stepkids in the mix, it makes for a hell of a crowd when we all get together."

"Sounds like it. How many siblings do you have?"

"Five."

Mike whistled and zipped up the insulated bag. "Quite the menagerie."

It was. And yet, for so much of his life, he'd felt lonely as hell.

Settling back against the counter, he lifted a shoulder.

Mike rested a hip next to him, not near enough to touch.

Unfortunate. He wanted to close the distance between them. Not in Mike's mom's kitchen, but soon.

"Easy to get lost in a crowd," Mike said softly. "Expectations that went along with being the eldest, too, I bet."

Daniel jolted. Had his face given that away? Or was Mike that perceptive? He turned and shifted closer. "It's not something people always consider."

"Being a twin, I have the same thing happen. The number of times I've had friends try to guess what it's like and to get it wrong... Especially since Maggie and I are fraternal."

"I guess you don't have the preternatural twin sense, then."

Mike laid a casual hand on Daniel's forearm. "No, it's the opposite. She and I can read each other's minds sometimes."

"Must be weird having her on a different continent."

"It is. And lately I can't help but feel like something is wrong." Mike shook his head. "She insists she's well. But she's not one to complain. She's got a real complex about making it seem like everything's fine, for my parents' sake and Cody's."

Daniel stroked his free hand down Mike's cheek. "Big dreams can mean big sacrifices."

"Yeah. Mine are so much smaller. Or at least, more local."

"Size doesn't matter with dreams, as long as they're yours."

Daniel's had been tied up with his family for long enough to blur the line between what he wanted and what he had to do to toe the Taylor line. How had he gotten to forty-four years of age without being clear on his own desires? And why was spending time with a man so much younger than him the catalyst to recognizing the issue?

Foolishness, all of it. His life wasn't set in stone, but it wasn't easily changed, either. He could stay quiet about his last name all he wanted, but it was going to cause issues. Damn, he wished it wasn't the case.

How long had it been since a man had caught his interest like this? *Years, maybe.* Certainly long enough to know it was damn rare to be so drawn in by the way a person laughed, to find every small part of him as fascinating as buried treasure. And the more he glanced around the Coopers' kitchen, the more he could guess that Mike's loving nature was linked in large part to his upbringing.

A collection of faded drawings was displayed on the fridge, along with a calendar covered in various colors of ink, all fixed to the surface with a collection of mismatched magnets. "Cody's quite the artist, I see."

"He's quite the kid," Mike said. "As much as Maggie being gone makes things busier and more complicated, I'm luckier for having him with me."

"That's…great."

Great for Mike and Cody, but not so much for Mike and *Daniel*, were they to decide to keep seeing each other after Daniel got his truck back and left town. Something told him

Bronco and Tenacity weren't close enough for a person caring for a kid to manage a long-distance relationship.

He startled at the thought. As if Mike was expecting to see Daniel again after he returned to Bronco. Except…maybe he'd want to? The other man wasn't treating Daniel like someone temporary. A person didn't take a one-and-done on a picnic or let him into his home, let him interact with his kid.

Daniel let out a breath. Mike Cooper was a damn puzzle. Nothing like the men who usually drew him in.

Maybe that was a good thing. Maybe he needed someone different.

Oof. He was getting ahead of himself. Once he worked the extent of his family's wealth into the conversation, Mike might not want anything to do with him at all.

His chest clenched at the thought.

Mike took a step closer and settled a hand on Daniel's hip. "It's nice you understand what Cody means—"

The screen door squawked.

A woman with dark brown hair and Mike's kind eyes bustled into the kitchen, a box full of groceries in her arms. "Michael, honey, thought you'd have left by now."

She shot Daniel a curious smile.

"Mom, hey." Mike jerked away from their near embrace and strode to take the box and put it on the counter. His eyes were wide as they flicked from his mom to Daniel. "We were about to leave. Do you need me to bring in the rest first?"

"Your dad's got it." Her heel clicks were all business as she approached Daniel and held out her hand. "Mike mentioned he'd invited a friend out to our ranch. I'm Ellen Cooper, and I promise we in no way intended to crash your date."

"Not a date, Mom," Mike grumbled. "This is my friend Danny."

"Absolutely a date, Mrs. Cooper," Daniel corrected with a grin as he accepted her handshake. "Nice to meet you."

"Nice to meet you, too." She smirked with all-knowing mischief. "I love being introduced to a man who's willing to distract my son for a few hours. Our operation wouldn't survive without him, but he deserves a little time to himself."

Mike's cheeks reddened. "Mom, come on."

"It's true," Mrs. Cooper said, turning to Daniel. "Did he tell you about our Maggie's adventure in South America? We couldn't be prouder of her but also of Mike for what he's doing with Cody to make it possible for Maggie to serve."

The pride in Ellen Cooper's tone was heartwarming.

"Health care is something you've passed onto your daughter, I hear?" Daniel asked.

"Yes, as much as I love the ranch—and as much as I'm ready to retire—I'll always be a nurse at heart," she said. "I think the nursing tradition will end with Maggie, though. Cody seems inclined to follow in his grandfather's and uncle's footsteps. And we can't blame him for falling in love with the land. Our son is a hell of a role model."

Looking like he wanted to dig a tunnel under the faded linoleum, Mike said, "Where is Cody? With Dad?"

Mrs. Cooper shook her head. "We left him in town with Payton and Adam after church. His best friends," she explained as an aside to Daniel. "Leaves you the whole afternoon to while away if you want, Michael. I'll pick him up in a few hours."

"I thought I'd show Danny the creek and the west pasture, get one last look at how the herd is doing before we shift them over the creek this week."

"If your calving season is on a similar schedule to ours, your calves are at the fun-to-watch age where they're playful," Daniel said, smiling at the promise of a good day.

Ellen's gaze turned thoughtful. "Mike mentioned you come from a ranching family. You're not one of *the* Taylors, are you? As in Taylor Beef?"

He bit back a curse. He didn't want to admit this to Ellen before he had the chance to hash it out with Mike. He also didn't feel right lying to a direct question.

"I mean, it is a common name," he hedged.

"Certainly," she replied.

"Not *that* common." Mike's expression was turning as hard as the granite countertops. Daniel hadn't imagined his warm smile could ever morph into something so stony and stiff. "Also doesn't seem like the kind of question requiring an evasive answer."

He froze. "Mike…"

"Can't deny it, can you?" He'd never heard Mike use such a bitter tone, not even when he was recounting some of Tenacity's tougher times.

"Well, I…"

"Just a regular guy, my ass."

Daniel's stomach turned. Mike's reaction was 100 percent his fault.

Ellen looked like she knew she'd poked a hornet's nest but wasn't quite sure how the swarm was going to react. "Should I not have asked?"

"No, you very much should have, Mom." Mike's emphasis dripped with disdain. "Quite the 'family business' you have, Danny. Let me show you mine. Not that it lives up to your high-class expectations. Let's go."

He grabbed a baseball cap off a peg on a coatrack and then stalked out the back door.

Daniel fisted his hands and fought the guilt and resignation roiling in his belly.

"Oh dear," Ellen whispered.

"Not your fault," he assured her, nodding a farewell. "And it was nice meeting you."

"I…yes. You, too, Danny." She looked confused about her son's abrupt departure.

Daniel gave her an awkward apology on his way out the door, unsure of if Mike's "Let's go" meant he'd be taking Daniel on the ride or would be dousing him headfirst in a horse trough.

Chapter Eight

"Mike, wait!"

Mike did not wait. He strode across the asphalt, heading for the door to the horse barn. A single set of footsteps followed him. His mom must have decided to give Danny and him their privacy.

"Hang on, please," Danny called. The thuds of his boots picked up to a jog, and he caught up to Mike right before he opened the side door. "I'm sorry. I screwed up the timing of things, and you're the one paying for it."

Mike went through the door, Danny on his heels. The second the door closed, he spun, flexing his hands in and out, in and out, trying to douse the anger in his veins.

Uncertainty flashed across Danny's too-handsome features. "Mike, hang on. I can explain—"

"Don't. Don't say a word," he cautioned. "I'm still too damn mad to hear whatever piss-poor excuse you have."

Danny leaned against the door and adjusted his Stetson, his gaze brimming with regret.

To his credit, he stayed silent for minutes while Mike paced.

But that was where the credit ended, because what a damn *liar.* Well, maybe not lying, exactly—Danny had never claimed *not* to be a Taylor—but he'd sure held some mighty important information to his chest. Not much mattered more than a person's roots. Hell, being a Taylor wasn't only about Danny being raised in the lap of luxury. He worked for Taylor Beef *now*, and the difference between that and Cooper Ranch meant he and Mike had virtually nothing in common.

Danny looked so miserable, though, frowning at the cement floor. His expression doused Mike's temper, enough for Mike to regain the ability to talk without yelling.

"I can't believe you played me like this," he croaked.

"I didn't…" Danny shook his head and swore. "You deserve an explanation. And then you'll want to take me back to town, I figure."

The implication being they'd say goodbye forever.

Mike freaking hated Danny's cloak-and-dagger routine, but he yearned for what this day *should* have been.

"Mike?" Danny ventured. "Do you *want* me to explain?"

"I honestly don't know."

As one of "those" Taylors, Danny was everything Mike had promised never to chase again. Yet another situation where he'd been drawn to a larger-than-life guy and ended up embarrassed.

Yet another situation where he was acting like an infatuated fool… Aiming high had always meant he shot far, far wide. The first few times, it had been embarrassing, but harmless. The same kind of high-school and college mistakes that everyone made. Not so much with Steven. After that humiliation, Mike thought he'd learned to be on the alert for wealthy assholes on the lookout for an easy target.

Did Danny see him that way, too? It hadn't felt like it. All the time they'd spent together had felt genuine, different from any man who'd previously caught his eye.

Then again, since when could he trust his feelings?

He needed to give Danny the chance to explain, if only to see if he could finally decipher a pattern for his relationship failures beyond having terrible romantic instincts.

"Who are you?" he muttered.

Danny slumped lower against the door. He sighed. "Rhetorical question, or do you want my life story?"

"Both."

Head tipping against the metal in resignation, Danny said, "Your mom was right. My dad and uncles own Taylor Beef. And I work for them. In the front office, though. My brothers and cousins will eventually take over the ranching operations."

Damn. Mike backed away a step.

"And you felt like you had to hide it from me. We barely know each other, and I find out you were keeping something crucial to yourself."

"I know. I was being selfish." Danny jammed his hands into his hair. "I miscalculated, badly. And I upset you, and I'm sorry."

"I'm not sure if an apology is enough."

"And that's your prerogative. I just—with a little time, I can explain better than I have. Could I have that chance? Please?"

Mike clenched his teeth hard enough to make his ears hiss.

The knee-jerk reaction would be a *no damn way.* But Danny seemed legitimately ashamed of his secrecy. And now that Mike knew who Danny really was, it would be easier to tell if the man was being dishonest.

"Fine," he grumbled. "Let's ride."

They barely spoke a word as they tacked up their horses. Danny required little direction aside from the location of the correct tack, but then, Mike would expect no less from a Taylor scion. He set Danny up with a stunner of an Appaloosa named Constellation, a ten-year-old mare who got along well with his own buckskin quarter horse, named the ever clever "Buck" by a four-year-old Cody.

And then they rode, cantering down a wide, flat path running parallel to a fence line.

Mike tried to keep his eyes directed forward but couldn't resist glancing at Danny. The man was born to be in the saddle. Long lines and an easy seat, a relaxed hand on the reins. Those goddamn work-of-art shoulders, rolling in time to the hoofbeats. That's what this afternoon should have been. The two of them, sharing a love for being on the back of a horse, having a few laughs over a simple meal.

As if a picnic could satisfy a Taylor.

Though he made do with fairground food last night.

And the Danny's ease around horses meant Mike couldn't claim they had *nothing* in common. Plus, the older man had been so good with Cody at the rodeo...

Argh. Why was he arguing on Danny's behalf?

They approached a small bridge, and Mike slowed Buck to a walk. Danny followed suit.

"Any iteration of 'I was going to tell you' sounds weak," Danny said.

Mike raised an eyebrow. "Or honest, depending on if and when you were planning to do just that."

"Today," he said.

If wishing made it so. "Convenient answer."

"Yeah, I can see why it's hard to take me at my word."

It was, but for some reason, Mike still wanted to believe the man.

"The thing is, Mike, I've been questioning my boundaries with my family for a while now. Especially with my dad. Moving off Triple T land was only the start. I've been resenting my job. Feeling like I needed something of my own, like it's time to be truer to myself. In my personal life, too—it's something I've struggled to do in romantic relationships. I haven't been able to get serious about anyone for a long time." He muttered a curse under his breath. "I'm not assuming we *will* get serious. But I didn't want to write it off."

"Okay, and I can see why you wouldn't share that with a person you just met, but you hid *everything* about who you are."

"I did." The admission came with a visible cringe. "I'll be

honest, a lot of the time when men know who I am or find out I'm wealthy, it's hard to know if they're interested in me or in my percentage share in Taylor Beef. And when you assumed I *didn't* have money and my alternator expenses would be tough to cover, it was refreshing." His smile was sad. "Of course, last night, I found out the opposite. Me having money is a major problem for you."

"My last boyfriend of mine was a rich prick," Mike replied, not bothering to sugarcoat the hard lesson he'd learned.

Danny winced. "Then you're right to be cautious."

"Yeah, I am." Cautious, and unwilling to fully open up to Danny about the facts of the breakup and his ex's deception. Sometimes it was necessary to keep his cards close to his chest.

Just like Danny's had to do, because of how he's *been screwed over by selfish people.*

They *definitely* had that in common…

"I wasn't sure what to do." Danny leaned forward and patted his horse's neck. "Keep hiding my background and in the process give you more evidence that rich folks are dishonest and untrustworthy. Or fess up and risk you writing me off immediately."

"So you went with option C? Let my mother suss you out and end up risking both things?"

"Seems so. And I deserve your reaction."

"Okay, but… I don't know how to reconcile the person I thought I was getting to know with the person you actually are. Upper management for Taylor Beef? Hell, one of the Taylor sons? As if you had to stick around waiting for your truck to get fixed. I bet you could afford to *buy* a tow truck to get your vehicle home, let alone the pittance it would cost you to hire someone to take it to wherever you live."

"Bronco Heights."

"Of course." Mike hoped his tone was closer to *resigned* than *derisive*, but he couldn't be sure.

"You're right," Danny admitted. "It would have been easy enough to get back home. My mom offered to come get me."

"And you didn't take her up on her offer because…"

"I wanted to stay. Because of you," his guest said simply.

Mike would have loved to say he didn't understand why, but somehow, he did. He'd felt the draw, too, the electricity between them. The curiosity pulling and tugging and nagging him to get to know every intricate facet of this man.

A tough task when said man had hidden one of the most important parts of himself.

Danny ran his free hand down his face. "You intrigued me, Mike. More than anyone has in a long time. So instead of calling for a rescue, I had you find me a place to crash."

"In three-star accommodation, no less."

Danny looked surprised, as if he hadn't been expecting anything close to a lighthearted response.

"Carol was already getting suspicious when she saw the color of my credit card, but then I was done for when I called down to the front desk on the off chance they provided robes."

Mike couldn't help but laugh. "Spoiled much?"

"Sometimes. Most of my tastes aren't so particular. I'd do a lot for the chance to show you."

"When? Aren't you planning to head home now that—"

Now that you've stopped trying to pull the wool over my eyes.

"No, at this point, I'll stay until my truck is done. I don't want to ask the inn for a refund." Danny cleared his throat. "And if you were up for spending more time together, despite my last name, I'd be a very thankful man."

What the hell was he supposed to believe?

Danny's explanation of wanting a break from the pressures of his job and that being anonymous for a night had been a welcome change did seem genuine. Just because the man had money didn't mean his life was easy, not with what he'd said about his relationship with his father. Mike could understand wanting to get away from reality now and again. And Danny's instincts had been right. Had he been upfront about being wealthy from the beginning, Mike wouldn't have given him the time of day. The guy had messed up, but not for malicious reasons.

His heart was telling him to forgive Danny for a very human mistake. But was seeing him again a good idea?

"I have a busy week," Mike said.

"Sure. I bet they all are." Danny paused, then blurted, "Your smile has been the highlight of my month. Having a beer with you made me feel more alive than I have in a long time. The rodeo, too. Seeing it through Cody's eyes—I haven't enjoyed one that much since I was a kid myself. And kissing you... I don't even know how to describe it. I'll take whatever time I can get with you. No expectations."

Hmm. With his responsibility for Cody, something strings-free made more sense anyway. A way to test out being with someone without risking his heart again.

"Some of life's best moments are more of an interlude than a main event," Danny said.

An interlude. With Danny—Daniel—Taylor.

"All right, then," Mike said. "No expectations, it is."

And with any luck, that would mean he'd avoid having his heart decimated like it had been the previous times he'd gotten involved with someone.

Danny's expression brightened enough to make the grass in the adjacent field grow a half an inch. "Really?"

"Yeah. I forgive you. If you could make sure I don't end up looking foolish for doing so, that'd be great."

"Mike—"

"Let's ride some more."

More talking might get him dangerously close to having *expectations.*

They signaled their horses to canter again and rode for another half hour until they got to the clearing by the creek where he'd wanted to have lunch. It didn't take them long to put back their sandwiches and cookies.

With the horses tied to the nearby fence and nibbling on some treats he'd brought for them, and not another human in sight except for the man stretched out next to him in a patch of grass, Mike let himself take a breath. He shrugged out of his work jacket, lay back and balled it behind his neck, closed his eyes and let the sun warm his face.

"Beautiful piece of land you've got here," Danny said as he lay beside him.

"Promise me you won't try to buy it off my dad."

"Um, sure." Danny's confusion was obvious. "I'm looking at places in North Dakota, not Tenacity."

"I'm going to consider that a promise," Mike mumbled. "We've had enough people sniffing around, looking to absorb properties or take over without prioritizing Tenacity's needs."

"Ah," Danny said, sounding like he'd figured something out. "How about I allay your worries. I'm not here to strike a deal with your dad, Mike. I'm not here for business at all."

The grass rustled as Danny shifted on Mike's right. A hand trailed up his arm.

Mike's eyes flew open and he took in the bluest, most hopeful gaze he could ever remember seeing.

"Is this okay?" Danny asked. He'd dropped his Stetson to the side and his hair was adorably rumpled.

Mike jerked his head in a single nod. "Seems the whole point of 'no strings' is to enjoy each other."

"It's not *not* the point. Or at least, it's one of them." Danny's palm played across Mike's chest.

"I'm willing to have you break it down for me."

"Nice and slow?" Lips teased his earlobe.

"Maybe not too slow." Mike clutched Danny's waist with

one hand and his shoulder with the other. Soft lips nibbled Mike's jaw, and he gasped. His fingers tightened, his body spinning away from him even though he was lying on the firm ground.

"Ungh." He couldn't manage a more coherent response.

"I very much wanted to see your ranch—" Danny's mouth traveled down Mike's neck "—because it matters to you. Not because I'm masterminding some nefarious plot to steal it from you."

The words were lighthearted. Mike suspected Danny might have used a different tone had he known someone *had* tried to use Mike to get to Cooper land. But damn it, the hot press of Danny's lips on his throat made it impossible to want to hash out his past embarrassments.

So long as *this* wasn't a mistake.

And as long as he kept his feelings out of it, it wouldn't be.

Teeth nipped over Mike's pulse, and he groaned.

"You make a convincing argument." Digging a hand into the soft, short waves at the back of Danny's head, Mike brought their mouths together. It was too easy to keep exploring, trailing his other hand along the hard back muscles covered by soft cotton, and then lower, to warm denim.

Danny shifted, an elbow on the grass, his chest touching Mike's side. The sun haloed his head, a golden glow edging his dark, fallen-angel hair.

God, if Mike's younger self had known this was in his future…

"Gotta admit, I like being your Cooper Ranch tour guide," Mike confessed.

"And what am I going to get a tour of, Mike?"

"Isn't there a checklist for how to fool around in the back forty?"

"If there is, I'm not in on the secret." Danny traced a finger down Mike's nose, then zigzagged over his mouth, landing in a ticklish tease in the divot above his lip.

"Me, either. Not a lot of queer men my age to pursue around here."

"Tenacity's dating pool is shallow?"

"To say the least. I did have a moment in a hayloft with a girl during my senior year, but only managed to prove I didn't want to be in a hayloft with a girl at all."

Danny chuckled. "I had a similar revelation at one point. Took a while to talk to my family about being gay, too. Hell, my dad still has a hard time believing it."

"Um, what? What's there to *believe*?"

Danny made a face, as if he was regretting bringing it up. Mike would put a pin in that question.

"So long as *you* know who you are," Mike said.

"I do. I also know where I want to be right now."

"Here?"

Hot lips traced another path down Mike's throat. "Exactly here."

"Uncle Mike, the pancakes are burning again."

The spatula hit the floor as Cody's warning jolted Mike from an intense daydream about the hour he'd spent by the river with Danny yesterday, talking and kissing. Nothing more—on the off chance one of the ranch hands had been out checking fences, he hadn't wanted to be caught with his pants literally around his ankles. He snatched the plastic flipper off the floor and gave it a quick wash before using it to take out the blackened pancakes and toss them into the garbage.

He turned down the element and then scooped three more blobs of batter into the skillet. If he didn't get his act together, Cody would be late for school. Not a great way to start the week.

But yesterday… Man, those moments with Danny had been the perfect way to end the weekend.

"Your smile is weird, Uncle Mike," Cody said from his perch on "his" chair at the small table by the kitchen window.

The house Mike had built for himself wasn't huge—three bedrooms, with an open-concept kitchen and living area. But it was big enough for him and his nephew, and after six months of Monday mornings with the boy, he was getting used to the questions and narration instead of the silence he'd lived with when he'd been roommate-less.

"*You're* weird," he teased, reaching over to tickle his nephew's side, earning a silly cackle.

He managed to flip the pancakes before they charred.

"I can't wait to tell my teacher about the dinosaur Danny won for me," Cody said. "And about all the junk food we ate and the barrel racing. The Hawkins Sisters were so cool. And I want to know if Payton and Adam got more than three bull's-eyes on the baseball toss. They're better at throwing than me, but I think I did pretty good."

Mike scooped two pancakes onto a plate and slid it in front of Cody. He and Cody had entirely different highlights from their evening at the rodeo. Danny winning the stuffed animal, yeah, but not for the sake of the prize, for getting to watch Danny's muscled arms flex. For the heated smile the man had flashed Mike whenever Cody's attention had been directed elsewhere. For their hint of a kiss…

Yesterday, they'd more than made up for the fleeting quality of the one they'd shared at the rodeo. Mike could still feel Danny's lips on his jaw, his neck, his mouth.

"You're doing it again, Uncle Mike. You look all foggy, like Mom does when she's reading pirate books."

Mike choked on a laugh. "You'll have to ask your teacher if she went to the rodeo. Most of Tenacity was there."

"Maybe. I didn't see her." Cody made a sloppy happy face on each pancake out of syrup, then dug in. He was half done chewing when he asked, "Are you acting all strange because of Danny? Do you like him?"

Mouth gaping, Mike fought his scrambling thoughts. His nephew caught on to more than the grown-ups in his life gave him credit for. And Mike supposed he hadn't been subtle about his interest in the older man.

"He's my friend, Cody. He's a nice guy," Mike hedged.

"Yeah, but you kissed him when I was on the bouncy slide," Cody said around another bite.

How had his nephew noticed something so brief? Good grief. "Chew with your mouth closed, kid."

Cody swallowed and grinned. "It's okay if you like him. I heard Grandma talking on the phone with Auntie Carol yesterday. She said you came back from riding horses with him looking like you'd taken a roll in the hay. What does that mean?"

Mike coughed. "That it, uh, looked like I fell off my horse."

Cody's eyes widened. "Did you?"

"No."

"So why—"

"Eat your pancakes. The school bus will be here in seven minutes."

Good grief. He was going to have to have a talk with his mom about what she was saying in Cody's vicinity.

And maybe, if he was lucky, he *would* get the chance to "roll in the hay" with Danny Taylor.

Chapter Nine

Monday night at Tenacity Social Club didn't look all that different from Friday or Saturday afternoon but for the lighting being a bit lower and a different set of faces. Daniel sat at the end of the bar, perpendicular to most of the room. Gripping the lowball glass that held most of a finger of bourbon, he tried not to be too obvious about his attempts to catch the bartender's eye.

Mike was busy pouring a pitcher of lager for a quartet of early-thirty-something cowboys over by the dartboard.

Daniel tried not to think too hard about how the younger men were closer to Mike's age than he was himself. When they were alone, it was easy to forget that more than fifteen years separated them. Out in public, it was harder to avoid reality: One of the cowboys whooping it up over a friend's bull's-eye might have more to offer Mike.

Still, the bartender had eagerly agreed to a few days enjoying each other's company. And they'd *definitely* enjoyed making out by the Coopers' creek.

It might require some creativity to etch out another moment where they could enjoy themselves more—it would be complicated with Cody living with Mike, and were Daniel to bring Mike to the inn, all of Tenacity would know by the time the clock struck midnight.

He'd satisfy himself with a conversation across the bar,

however interrupted it was given Mike needing to tend to his crowd.

A number of the tables were filled, and a handful of people were two-stepping to one of Beyoncé's country songs. Looked like fun. It had been a while since he'd gone for a spin around a dance floor. The opportunities had been few and far between.

A set of strong arms, muscles highlighted by a rolled-cuff short-sleeve T-shirt, crossed on the bar in front of him. "Still thirsty?"

He fixed his gaze on Mike's sultry stare. "What are the chances we could join in the dancing?"

Mike winked. "Sorry, gorgeous, but I can't leave the bar."

Daniel hadn't expected a different answer, but part of him was still disappointed. "I get it. Better to be safe."

Mike shook his head. "No, we are safe here. I mean, I know there's always the possibility someone would take offense to me dancing with another guy. There were a few times in college when I felt the need to fly under the radar. Damn scary, when it happens. It won't here, though. I know these folks and they know me. I wouldn't be worried."

"I'm glad."

Leaning a little closer, Mike lifted a corner of his mouth. "Not to say we wouldn't cause a stir if we tried out a two-step. But it would be more because of gossip than because of people disagreeing with our right to love each other."

Daniel blinked. He couldn't stop his jaw from dropping. *To what, now?*

Though, given time, how farfetched would the assumption be?

Mike winced. "I didn't—damn. I meant… Showing interest. Dating. *Dancing* with each other."

Daniel ran a hand over Mike's crossed forearms. "I know what you meant. And I'm not bothered if people see us together and their tongues start wagging, as long as they aren't being malicious."

"There isn't much malice in Tenacity. I grew up here. It's rare I'm treated with anything but respect. And I control the flow of beer a few nights a week, so..." He straightened, holding his hands out as if to say *What are they going to do about it?*

Letting out a short laugh, Daniel took a drink of his bourbon. It wasn't as smooth as the vintage he had in his liquor cabinet at home, but he welcomed the burn. "I've run the gamut of places, from the ones where I knew I'd better keep my mouth shut about being gay to the ones where I can openly kiss a man. I have solid instincts, but it's good to get assurance from a local."

"From a local who would love nothing more than to dip you on the dance floor," Mike said with a bashful smile. "Of course, if I did, you wouldn't be able to walk down the street without someone asking you about me. I'm sure my mom's phone would be a mess of texts and nosy calls."

Going off the few tidbits Mike had revealed about his past, the last time he had dated someone from out of town, it had ended poorly. Daniel's levity faded. His time with Mike *would* end. They were from different worlds. But if they were careful, they could avoid the animosity Mike still held from his last relationship.

"It would be the same for me if we were in Bronco," Daniel said. "Like I mentioned yesterday, my dad's got his head in the sand about my sexuality, which means I don't often take my boyfriends home."

Mike's face turned stormy. "Your family really doesn't support you?"

"No, my mom does, and my brothers and sisters. My dad isn't openly antagonistic. It's more he's stubborn as his prize bull and can't see outside his own experience... Not to make excuses for him. It's not right. He just can't seem to make sense of his oldest son not wanting a wife." He sighed. "Part of me thinks I should give him an ultimatum—accept me or I'll walk away. But my sisters did that, for a variety of reasons, and it didn't make them happy. If I stay, I risk him thinking he's in the right, as much as we've all gotten better about telling him he's not. If I leave, I'm giving up the world I've always known. The family I care about, very much. Either way, I'm the one who loses. So as much as he's thoroughly wrong, it's not easy to know what to do. Nor is it something I want to bring a partner into. I don't regret creating the boundary, but it's made it hard to find commitment."

"I'm not here to criticize the strength of your boundaries, Danny," Mike said, voice low enough it was almost hard to hear him over the music and chatter. "I'm betting you've done the best you could with what you've had at any given time. But I am sad you don't have unconditional support. Especially coming from your dad. I don't know what I'd do without mine. I'm sorry yours is choosing ignorance."

"Thanks." Envy rose, twisting with the pleasure of being understood. What would it have been like to grow up in a family like Mike's where joy and laughter ruled the dinner table, not the strict expectations of being a Taylor?

A waitress entered an order into the point of sale at the other end of the bar, and the small drink-order machine hummed to life.

Mike glanced at it before twining his fingers with Daniel's and squeezing. "It really is the bartending getting in the way of a dance. There's no one else to pour drinks tonight."

"I know. Another time."

Daniel spent another hour at the bar, his attention drifting between the two televisions above the rows of bottles on the backsplash—one with playoff hockey, one with baseball. But always back to the glorious mop of hair he'd explored yesterday and wanted to explore again. Mike came over to chat when he could, given the crowd kept him busy for a lot of the time.

After finishing his second bourbon, Daniel rose from his stool.

Mike's face fell. "You're taking off?"

"Two's my limit on a Monday. And I assume with Cody, you have to get home after your shift."

"Yeah, my mom'll be looking to get to bed," Mike said. "Cody stays at my parents' place if I work on Friday or Saturday, but she hangs out at my place when I have a late shift on a school night."

"Want to do something together tomorrow?"

"I wish." Mike frowned into the Coke he was pouring from the soda gun. "I have to be up before the sun. I don't always do ranch work the morning after a shift here, but tomorrow I have to. We're moving the herd to the pasture across the creek."

"Want help?" Daniel offered.

Mike looked taken aback. "Really?"

"Yeah. I know I'm an office stiff, but I still know my way around cattle."

"I… Yeah. That'd be great. Come out for six—" Mike paused. "Damn, you don't have a truck."

"Well, the mechanic said—"

"I'll come get you."

Daniel was *technically* without his vehicle. The mechanic had called him right before closing time to say the repairs were completed. But he hadn't made his way over to the shop to get it, figuring he'd do it in the morning. And he still could, after he helped the Coopers. For now, getting a ride from a big-hearted, good-looking cowboy sounded like the best luck he'd ever had.

"You sure know how to sweeten an offer," Daniel said with a grin.

* * *

Before dawn on Tuesday, Mike pulled his truck under the covered driveway in front of the inn's entrance. He checked his reflection in the visor mirror to make sure his hair hadn't taken on a life of its own after his shower, then his texts to see if Danny had replied to the I'm on my way heads-up he'd sent.

Danny: I'm almost ready. See you soon

His heart tripped, triple speed.

Before he got the chance to calm the hell down, there was a quiet knock on the passenger window. The door opened, and Danny slid in, bearing two travel cups of rich smelling coffee.

"I know you said you like tea more, but Carol insisted."

"Prefer, yes, but I'll drink anything with caffeine in it at this time in the morning." Mike held his right arm out sideways and made a grabby-hand gesture.

Chuckling, Danny slotted one mug into the console, handed Mike the other and leaned in. "You must be exhausted, sweetheart."

Mike fell into the kiss. He *was* tired. But his passenger's tender greeting gave him a jolt not even the caffeine from the aromatic brew could match.

"Has the inn upgraded their in-room coffee makers?" Mike asked, taking a long swig as soon as Danny eased back into his seat.

"No, your godmother took pity on me and sneaked me some from the pod machine the staff use. Said she wouldn't do it for anyone *but* her godson. Gave me quite the look when I explained where I was headed at this hour."

Mike let out a joking *pshaw.* "She should know there won't be time for fooling around on herding day."

"That and she already knew where I was going—apparently she'd already been texting your mom, who's at your house?"

Oh, good grief. "Yeah, Mom gets Cody ready for school on the mornings I'm working." He shook his head. "I didn't realize she and Carol were discussing my dating life before the sun was even up, though."

"Maybe it's because Carol has skin in the game, what with me staying under what she considers her roof."

"Ha, yes, she'll adopt any weary traveler she thinks needs a home."

"I have a home, Mike," Danny said softly. "Might not have built it on ranch land with my own hands like you did yours, but it's still mine."

Yeah, Danny had a home, on one of the fancier streets in Bronco Heights, he'd confessed over one of his bourbons last night. But from what he'd said about his family, he had mixed feelings, especially with his dad. It seemed like overreaching so early on in their friendship or situationship or whatever it was they were developing, but if days like today could give Danny a sense of place and belonging, even for a few moments, then Mike needed to do more than wrangle cattle before he went to bed tonight.

Mike took Danny's free hand and squeezed, then brought it to his lips to kiss Danny's thumb. "I know where you come from." *Too well.* "But you don't seem anxious to return to it."

"No, I guess I haven't been. Probably can't blame your mom and Carol for gossiping about how I've been lingering in Tenacity."

"I have a feeling the messages flying back and forth have more to do with the time you and I are spending together." He turned onto the highway for the short drive to the ranch. "Is your mom like this?"

Danny's cheeks reddened. "Has she interfered in my love life, you mean? She very well might have, had I given her the chance."

"Why does it have to be past tense? You have plenty of time."

"Says the man who's sixteen years my junior." Danny's rueful chuckle filled the cab.

"Yeah, well… Kissing has a way of making those years irrelevant."

"Kissing, you say? Here I thought I was coming out to your ranch to do some heavy lifting."

Mike glanced to the passenger side long enough to wink. "I'm a full believer in maximizing the hours in a day."

It took them over an hour to get to the ranch, ready the horses and ride out to the pasture where the cattle were grazing. They joined a small but efficient group—two ranch hands led by Mike's dad, Larry.

Most mornings, the sunrise and the sweet spring weather would hold Mike's attention, but who cared about a pastel-washed sky when there was a dark and handsome cowboy to surreptitiously check out? He hadn't factored in traditional cattle-wrangling gear when he'd prepared himself for the sight of Danny Taylor on a horse.

Chaps. Damn.

They were utilitarian. An old set of Mike's dad's, but still good enough to make for an easier ride and a layer of protection.

But damn, Mike would be dreaming for a long while about what the worn brown leather did to Danny's legs.

Strong, lean. In line with what the man's work jacket did to his shoulders. Danny had worn the garment a few times now. Made Mike suspect his guest had a suitcase full of business clothes with him, limiting what he could wear for ranch work. If Danny had been planning to survey real estate in North Dakota, it wouldn't have been a Carhartt-and-Levi's situation, not for a Taylor.

And if the heaps of eye candy weren't enough, there was hearing Danny talk over the plan for moving the cattle.

"And here I thought an operation like the Triple T would have to use ATVs, given the size," Larry commented, showing his surprise after Danny had shared the similarities between the Taylors' operation and Cooper Ranch's practices.

"No, sir," Danny said. "My dad's a proud member of the 'calm steers taste better' club. Never wants to risk our product quality. We'll be using horses to move cattle until the last Taylor is six feet under."

"I suppose you don't get superrich without knowing a thing or two about how to run a business," Mike said. "It isn't all cutting corners and dominating the little guy?"

Danny raised an eyebrow. "I'd hope it's not about manipulative dealings at all. It's one of the reasons I'm needed—herd management for a ranch the size of the Triple T requires a big staff. I'm the one who hires them and organizes their training. I don't do a lot of the fieldwork, but I need to intimately understand each step of what happens on the ground, to make sure I'm hiring qualified hands. My brothers drag me out a few times a year, mainly to harass me about getting rusty."

Intimately. Mike's brain was deep in the gutter if it chose to latch on to that particular word.

Then again, each little fact he gleaned from Danny made him want "intimate understanding" of his own. And not solely physical. Danny's smile carried a weight Mike felt in his soul. This man was on the verge of sliding right into Mike's heart and binding some of the jagged edges.

It made Mike darn sad over the obvious jagged edges Danny was carrying around himself.

When it was time to start moving the herd, Mike's dad gave them their instructions. The lead ranch hand, Harold, was on foot, leading one of the older, calmer animals. Mike started the slow, stalking sweep to encourage the cattle to bunch. Between the mamas and their growing babies, they had about two-hundred animals to keep track of and drive to the longer grass.

The animals picked up on his movements and tightened the distance between themselves. It was a fine balance between using their herd instinct to get them to move and stressing them out. Once they started to follow Harold, Larry took one side, Danny the other. A younger ranch hand trailed behind, ready to move the temporary electric fencing.

Like he'd been born in a saddle, Danny guided his horse at a masterful speed. Mike, in behind, had his own horse to watch as well as the slow-moving herd, but his eyes kept getting drawn to the low-set cowboy hat and the strong, gloved hand with an easy grip on the reins.

If Mike let himself contemplate that hand any more, he'd be thinking of things far beyond kissing. Shaking his head, he focused on his task.

For hours.

Every shift of the cattle pulled his eyes to the left side of the herd, to cotton hugging strong shoulders, to the studied pinch of Danny's cheeks. Sunglasses hid the secrets in his dark eyes, but the tension in his jaw and the crinkles next to his temples spoke of being deep in thought.

His mouth was relaxed, though. Even his carved-from-marble lips, more suited to admiration in an Italian square than a field in Montana, weren't caught up in whatever close analysis Danny was performing on the animals.

They were just curved in enjoyment.

Mike knew the patience it took to care for animals this way, and it was the second gut check of the day.

Danny Taylor loved being on the back of a horse, out in the field, no matter how long it took to coax the herd from one patch of spring grass to the next. Cooper Ranch being the equivalent of a single square to the vast quilt of the Taylor holdings didn't seem to faze the man.

The surprise Mike had felt over the Taylors holding similar beliefs about animal husbandry exposed an uncomfortable assumption of his own.

Danny's easy acceptance of and respect for the size of Cooper Ranch made Mike like the man even more. Everything about the man was too easy to like. To *more than* like.

Caution squeezed his throat. Going too fast with Danny was tipping him into the same territory he always ended up in, with him head-over-heels for someone who ended up being a bad match. He especially had to avoid becoming the same heartbroken mess he'd been after Steven. He'd swathed himself in a necessary protective layer, and it would be foolish to shed it after a handful of days.

Chapter Ten

For all Danny was chill as they worked, Mike's thoughts made it hard for him to follow suit.

Hours of sweeping the suspicious herd and then moving fencing would normally clear his head. Not around six feet of perfection on a horse, though. And not when said perfection was everything he'd been telling himself to steer clear of for so long.

It was too damn hard to tell if the red flags he had trained himself to look for were actual issues or figments of his need to protect himself.

God, he was way too in his head about it all. Talk about the perfect way to complicate what should have been a simple, enjoyable day.

As soon as they finished erecting the fences and confirmed a final head count, he went over to where his dad was standing with Danny. Both men had thoughtful looks on their faces, though a great deal of fatigue pulled at Larry's as well.

"What would I do if I was running a smaller ranch?" Danny asked, seeming to repeat something Larry had said.

Larry nodded.

Mike had to fight from showing the immediate gut clench of his dad asking for advice.

"Bottom line's been getting redder," Larry said. "We're down to a skeleton staff. After we sold some of our animals, we had to let some hands go, too."

Mike coughed. "Is this a conversation we should be having with a—" *Stranger.*

He caught himself before he used the word. Aside from being rude—he was the one who had invited Danny out, for heaven's sake—Danny wasn't here to case Cooper Ranch for purchase. No part of Mike wanted to believe Danny was here to screw him over.

Larry and Danny both stared at him.

"A competitor," he supplied. *Weak sauce, Cooper.*

Larry laughed. "I doubt they see us as competition, son."

Mike rubbed the back of his neck, shooting his dad a look. He knew he sounded off base. Just because his gut warned him to be on the alert didn't mean he needed to run with the feeling. He could set it aside and *enjoy* this man for whatever fleeting amount of time he stayed in town.

Danny studied Mike with careful eyes before turning his attention to Mike's father. "You're running into issues at auction?"

"Who isn't?" Larry said.

"Probably Taylor Beef," Mike tried to joke.

Danny looked a bit rueful. "I'm not going to claim we're facing the same kind of vulnerability, but falling beef prices force us to think creatively, too."

The discussion continued as they mounted their horses and rode back to the barn. Danny ran Larry through a few possibilities, different ways calving could be scheduled in order to stagger when the animals got to market and some possible adjustments to feed. Their guest listened, too.

His comments weren't calculated or to stroke his own ego but to give Mike's dad some solid advice. Danny threw out both sympathy and some concrete suggestions he had seen work on other small ranches.

He was smart.

He was *kind.*

His expression was without artifice, his hands easy on the reins as he led Constellation past the paddock toward the barn.

Sheer want swept over Mike. He had to check his seat to avoid toppling off his own horse. Gritting his teeth, he slowed Buck to an easy walk.

When Larry reached the round driveway between the two barns and the paddock, he pulled back gently on the reins.

Danny followed suit, leaning forward to stroke the paint's neck. "Atta girl. Good girl."

Another swirl of heat blurred Mike's sanity. That tone... Damn.

All right. Enough, now. His reactions were so out of line, reading in sexual meaning where there wasn't anything. But it was easy to imagine what it would be like to get praise from Danny Taylor, and it was something he craved at his core.

Figuring his cheeks were redder than the stain on the barn, he lowered the brim of his hat and busied himself with getting off his horse.

"Let me know if you want to talk more about any of it, Larry. I could send you some resources, too," Danny said, swinging a long leg over his saddle and easing to the ground.

"I appreciate it, Danny. Generous of you to give us your time today. In more ways than one," Larry said before dismounting and guiding his chestnut toward the smaller barn.

Mike called out a goodbye to his dad and motioned for Danny to follow him to the other barn.

Danny stayed put, one hand holding the short lead rope, the other jammed into one of the back pockets of his jeans.

Raising a brow, Mike said, "Not in a hurry to get cleaned up?"

"Might be crowded in the barn, and I'd rather be..." He sighed. "What were you really going to say?"

Nerves tightened around Mike's throat. "Just now? Nothing."

"No, earlier, when your dad asked me for advice. You called me your competitor. But that wasn't your first thought."

Crossing his arms, Mike rested them on the seat of his saddle. Felt safer to have the animal between them. *Stranger* was harsh, inaccurate. There was a reason he'd stopped himself before speaking it aloud. It said more about Mike than Danny.

And though Mike didn't know *what* he wanted Danny to be, it wasn't a stranger.

"I'd love to pretend I don't have hang-ups, but I do," he said, figuring out a way to soften the truth. "And they're not fair to you. I invited you here. You've been nothing but kind to help us. To answer my dad's questions, too."

"You're struggling to trust me." Danny's assertion was barely a murmur.

"I don't trust the person I assumed you would be, if that makes any sense," Mike said. "The last time I got involved with a man who was giving my dad advice, it didn't end well. He nearly had me convinced my dad should sell."

"As long as you can see I'm *not* him." Danny took a step closer. "I'm not here to hurt your dad or to cause problems in Tenacity. Your town has enough going on without some outsider interfering. Nothing I suggested to your dad was off base, was it?"

"No. It was helpful. You're—" *So damn smart.* "You know the business."

"I would hope so." The following grin was enough to take a man out at the knees.

Mike's chest ached. "By inviting you here, I wanted to prove I'm starting to let it all go."

To find something new.

Thankfully he was able to keep *that* part of the truth in.

"You don't need to prove anything to me, Mike. We all walk through life dragging a whole-ass history behind us, and sometimes it makes us move slow." Danny slid off his sunglasses and slipped them into the front pocket of his shirt, and for the first time in hours, nothing stood between Mike and the heat in those dark brown eyes.

"I…" Damn, how was a person supposed to be anything but weak under such an onslaught? Mike gripped the horn and cantle of the saddle, on the verge of earning a dirty look from Buck for leaning on him too hard. He silently cursed his empty water canteen because damn, his throat was dry.

Danny shook his head. "Maybe it is time to clean up after all." Without another word he led Constellation into the barn.

After cooling Buck down and tending to his coat, hooves, food and water, Mike slung the saddle on the pegs in the tack room.

Before he could turn, a hand landed between his shoulder blades. Light-but-firm pressure pushed his chest against the leather seat. Danny's other hand palmed the shiplap wall, just past the saddle. A kiss teased Mike's neck, nuzzling from his earlobe down to his shirt collar.

He melted.

Danny's tongue traced a hot line.

A low, needy sound escaped Mike's throat.

The fingers on his back splayed, holding him in place. Danny tossed Mike's hat onto a bench and slid his palm along Mike's belly, right above his belt buckle.

"Mmm." Mike couldn't keep the sound in.

"I'm guessing this room isn't super private," Danny lamented.

"No." Mike put a hand over the one teasing his shirt up. "But I'm having a hard time caring."

A muttered curse tickled his ear. "The feel of you, Mike… You're…"

The groan Danny let out was everything he needed to know.

Mike eased the other man's hand down to the growing bulge behind his fly. *Damn. Yes.* That's what he wanted. Danny's fingers tensed, riding the line between a tender caress and a tantalizing grip.

Mike nearly fell apart.

"I want to say screw the risk of someone walking in," he said thickly, "but I can't."

"No problem. We can—"

Danny went to tug his hand away, but Mike held the long, work roughened fingers in place.

"*Wait*. We can risk it a little longer."

He kept his own hand still, guaranteeing his pleasure for a few more precious seconds. He pressed his back against the solid wall of muscle and heat behind him. A quick shift of his hips proved he wasn't the only one straining against his jeans. Danny was hard as hell, too, pretty much perfect, sandwiched against Mike's ass.

Danny's swallow was audible. "Touching you is a damn privilege."

Temptation burned in his veins. "Oh my God, you can't just say stuff like that."

"Why?"

"Because it'll make me beg you to go exploring, and I'll be right on the edge when the door will open and someone will barge in and catch me in the middle of losing my ever-loving mind."

"On the edge, hmm?"

"Yes. But it's already two o'clock, and I need to get you back to town before the school bus arrives, and—*argh*."

Twisting away from Danny's embrace, he shifted to the side, creating a few necessary feet of space. His gaze landed on the man who had him close to ruin. The need churning in those dark eyes made Mike's already shaky knees threaten to give out.

"Not the most convenient time, then," Danny teased.

"And aren't you picking up your truck soon?"

"Yes," Danny said. "You worried about me skipping town?"

His instinct was to shrug, to hide how much the thought scared him. He also knew his reaction wasn't rational. He could be honest with Danny.

"You wouldn't go without saying goodbye," Mike said.

Danny stepped closer again and caught Mike's elbow with a gentle hand. He leaned in. "You're right, I wouldn't. I'm not one for unfinished business."

"I like a thorough man."

"I don't want you to think we have to rush into bed, though. As much as I'd love to go there with you, maybe it isn't meant to be?" Danny mused.

It looked like he was trying to keep the disappointment off his face.

"We will. After I figure out when I'm free." Mike stepped close enough to give the other man a gentle, reassuring kiss. "Because for me, it doesn't feel like rushing."

It felt *necessary*.

If he didn't find the moments he'd need to explore this feeling, this need with Danny, he'd never forgive himself.

Daniel lay in his bed at the hotel on Wednesday morning— alone, sadly, but such was life—and grinned at his phone.

A picture of his jacket, hanging from the hook in the crew cab of Mike's truck, followed the text.

Mike: Look familiar?

He *had* forgotten his jacket, and he didn't regret it one bit.

Daniel: I'll drive out to get it after I pick up my truck this morning

Mike: All good, I can bring it in with me

Mike: My shift at the club starts at noon

Mike: Unless you're leaving before then

Mike: Please don't leave

Mike: Without saying goodbye! My thumb slipped. Pressed send early

Mike: And for some reason, I'm all over spamming you with my chaos. Ignore the above. I can bring your jacket into town, unless you're leaving before my shift starts, in which case I'll leave it on my parents' porch. I'm out checking fences this morning. Would rather be sleeping

Screw wild horses—a herd of bison couldn't drag Daniel out of town without a goodbye.

Or maybe at all.

Damn. That was foolishness, right there. He needed to stop before it cemented into his brain.

Mike's awkwardness tugged at his heart and at the corners of his mouth, and he typed: Meet you at the club at noon

Mike: If you come a bit earlier, we'll have privacy

Privacy. Yes, please. It was too easy to picture Mike's lean frame weighing down the mattress next to him. Of planting his lips along salt-tinged skin like yesterday.

Of not being worried about interruptions this time.

Forcing himself out of dreamland, he flicked through a backlog of messages.

Mom: Any updates on your truck?

Eloise: Would you call Mom? She's worried about you and is harassing the rest of us to compensate.

Seth: Why the hell aren't you home yet? If you're dragging your heels to get out of helping with branding, I will brand your ass

Seth: Unless you're bailing on North Dakota entirely

Seth: Thanks for that, by the way, jackass—I do not want to lose my realtor as a contact

Oof, Seth was salty this morning. Not unwarranted—he had been counting on Daniel to do the legwork on the real-estate deal during an otherwise busy spring ranching season—but he needed to chill. Daniel had things under control, like always.

Resisting the urge to tell all of them to go away, he shot his mom a brief *will keep you posted*, ignored his sister's plea and replied to Seth's terse collection of messages with an assurance the Realtor was understanding and had time to meet with Danny this coming Saturday and Sunday. With his truck ready to pick up, he *could* be home later this afternoon.

Something in his core protested at the thought.

He flipped back to his text history with Mike. Swinging by the club before it opened and having some time together where they wouldn't get interrupted sounded perfect.

He typed and sent, *See you before noon.*

Dropping his phone back onto the nightstand, he rolled onto his stomach and groaned a curse into his lumpy pillow. His hotel bed wasn't the picture of luxury. The comforter and sheets were serviceable but nothing like the ones he'd splurged on at home.

But if Mike were to get tangled up in them, they'd be perfection.

Was going to see the North Dakota property worth it? If he stayed in Tenacity until Sunday, it might earn him a weekend to while away the hours with Mike in this bed. If Seth was so hot to trot about making his Realtor happy, maybe he could be the one to make the long drive.

Daniel's chest tightened. If he changed his plans again, his dad and brothers were going to think he'd lost the plot. He'd spent months talking up his plan to explore new opportunities.

And whenever he thought of being back in the office, the craving still flared, impatient and itchy.

It'd been calm yesterday, though. His time out on the Coopers' ranch had felt like…enough. He'd moved cattle, given Larry advice and spent hours catching glances of Mike. Through it all, he'd felt settled.

And the calm enjoyment of working with Mike and his dad only compounded how he didn't feel that way when at his own job.

How *was* he going to leave Tenacity?

Chapter Eleven

Still mulling over how long he could stay in Tenacity before someone back home filed a missing-person report, Daniel took his time on the way to the mechanic.

Handing over his credit card to cover the repair made his heart sink further than he knew possible. Getting his truck back meant one fewer reason to stay.

Chuck passed him the full-page receipt, complete with details on what had been fixed.

"This'll get you where you need to go," the grizzled man said, "but you'll want to have your brake pads done soon. They're almost shot."

"Seriously? This truck isn't even two years old."

Chuck shrugged. "You've put a lot of miles on it. Sometimes you end up with a lemon."

"Will the brakes get me to North Dakota and back?"

"Yeah. You'll make it. You got a good mechanic in Bronco? Take it to them when you get home."

"Or you could do it for me," he said. "Not sure I like the sound of driving that far without functioning brakes."

"It's not an emergency—"

"Even so." He was already here. Might as well get them fixed just in case. "How long would it take you to get the pads in?"

"Not as long as the alternator. I could do it tomorrow, maybe Friday."

What was two days when it came to being safe on the road? "Sounds like a plan. I'll bring it back when you're ready to swap the pads out."

Chuck looked somewhat amused. "Didn't you say you were on your way out of state? You're wanting to stick around Tenacity for longer? Usually folks can't wait to get on the road when they stop here. Especially folks from places like Bronco."

Bronco doesn't have a bartender who makes my head—and my heart—spin.

A half hour later, he parked his truck in the inn's small lot and walked the short distance to the Tenacity Social Club. The charm of Central Avenue couldn't be denied. Some boarded storefronts, sure. But a number of businesses were resisting the financial downturn. Daniel bet it was due to the love of the town's residents. A bustling lunch crowd was visible through the windows of both the Silver Spur Café and Castillo's. The smell of grilled meat and chili peppers coming out of the latter had his mouth watering. In the time it took him to walk the few blocks, a number of people flowed in and out of Tenacity Feed and Seed, too.

For a sleepy small town, the place was hopping.

He even saw a familiar face.

Mike's best friend, the one they'd bumped into at the rodeo, was a half a block down from the Social Club, talking to a pair of women around her age. Jenna had her baby in a stroller, and the other women were fawning over the child.

He was about to descend the club's staircase when she noticed him and waved. Her gaze landed somewhere between hopeful and knowing.

He waved back, then made his way down to the basement level. His stomach skittered.

A country ballad played on the speakers. The place was

empty of patrons. No one to witness how damn excited he was to greet the man with his back to the door, polishing glasses behind the bar.

Mike turned. His face… *Wow*. No word for that expression but *joy*.

Daniel couldn't remember the last time his mere presence had earned an instantaneous burst of happiness from someone, and it made him feel like he was standing on the peak of a mountain, arms spread wide, wind in his face, a damn king at the top of the world.

"Hey there, sweetheart," he said, voice hoarse.

"You came." Mike dropped his polishing cloth and came from out behind the bar, meeting him in the middle of the floor. Digging his hands into Daniel's hair, Mike kissed with a bruising intensity.

Needing to steady himself, Daniel gripped at the denim and leather of Mike's jeans and belt, and returned the kiss. Heaven. When he'd woken up this morning, he'd hadn't realized this moment had been the whole point of getting out of bed, but here it was. With every shift of Mike's mouth on his, pleasure raced up his spine.

He tightened his hold on Mike's hips, pulling until their belt buckles scraped together. Heat washed over him, gripping him low, making him crave more pressure, more closeness. The light calluses on the heels of Mike's palms scraped his cheeks. A low moan rumbled against his lips.

Nothing sounded better than knowing this man wanted him with the same intensity churning through his own chest. The hardness behind Mike's fly hinted at the possibility.

He paused, taking a shuddering breath and resting his forehead against Mike's. "You're on the clock. We shouldn't get carried away."

Another low sound against his cheek, this one a groan of reluctant agreement.

"How about…" Mike took a deep breath and pressed a soft kiss right in front of Daniel's ear, eliciting a rush along his skin. "Is your offer for a dance still good?"

Daniel nodded.

Mike pulled his phone from his back pocket and futzed with something for a few seconds.

A blend of piano and steel guitar filled the room, followed by a masculine voice singing about the bar being empty and the bartender sweeping the floor. Brad Paisley's "We Danced." He knew the song well from his college years.

He couldn't help laughing at the perfection of the choice. "Just replace the woman in the song forgetting her purse with me forgetting my jacket in your truck."

"Exactly." Mike's expression was part soft vulnerability, part self-satisfaction. He slid his hands around Daniel's back until they rested low. "The barroom floor is empty… So, we dance."

"Cute, Cooper. Going to sing along, next?"

Pink spread on Mike's cheeks. "I can carry a tune."

Daniel kissed the corner of the flush, then trailed along the soft skin until nipping at the very tempting earlobe. It was right there, after all, and with the scent of apples coming off those delicious brown curls…

A short gasp puffed against his own ear.

With his hands on Mike's back and their cheeks pressed together, it was too easy to get pulled into the intimacy. Warmth tinged his chest, seeping through the cotton of his button-up shirt and the T-shirt covering Mike's hard pecs.

Being close, swaying to the familiar beat…

Keep it light.

"I'm surprised you thought of this song," Daniel said. "You were what, four or five when it came out?"

"Around there." Mike sounded a little embarrassed. "This album is one of my mom's favorites."

"Not sure how I feel about having more in common with your mom than you."

"I disagree," Mike said. "If anything, I keep getting blown away by how easy it is to spend time with you, which couldn't happen if we had nothing in common."

Blown away… That was it, all right. Daniel tightened his hold, soaking up the goodness of the weight of this man against his chest.

"Unless I'm alone in feeling that way," Mike continued, sounding almost shy.

"No. You're not alone." He couldn't stop the hint of a tremble in his words.

"Good."

It *was* good.

When the song switched to another slow, older country song that reminded Daniel of bumping along one of the Triple T's backroads in his first truck, an F-150 he'd bought off his uncle, he didn't ask whether or not Mike wanted to stop.

Thank God he'd bought himself two more days here. Maybe they'd even get the chance to have some time—

Mike jolted back.

Daniel startled. "What—"

A laugh rang out behind him, and he turned to face their new arrival.

"Oops," the familiar redhead said unapologetically.

"Jenna." Mike's eyes narrowed.

Mike's friend was holding her baby in her arms, and the stroller was nowhere to be seen. Mischief danced in her blue eyes.

Daniel nodded a greeting, which she returned with a smile.

"If I'd known your intentions when I saw you come down the stairs, I wouldn't have interrupted," she said.

"Yes, you would have," Mike grumbled.

"Maybe." She grinned. "But Robbie has something to show you."

The kid reached in Mike's direction, babbling, "Ma. *Ma. Maaaaa.*"

Jenna scoffed. "It's a good thing she said 'Mama' for me before she started calling you 'Ma.'"

Mike slid his hands into his back pockets with a shrug. "Robbie and I were always destined to be tight, Jen."

"Perils of her seeing your face before mine after she was born," Jenna said.

"Just for a second," Mike said. "She was in your arms almost immediately."

Huh? Daniel had so many questions.

His face must have broadcast his confusion because Jenna looked at him with dawning realization.

"Oh! Mike was in the delivery room with me."

Asking where her partner had been seemed a road full of potholes deep enough to swallow a tractor.

"I can see Mike being calm under pressure," Daniel said, settling on something safer.

The man in question rubbed the back of his neck and shot him an *aw shucks* half smile, decimating Daniel's self-control in the process. Was there no limit to the man's charm?

"He was," Jenna said. "With my husband gone, I needed a strong shoulder to lean on, and Mike's are some of the strongest around. He didn't miss one childbirth class and managed to convince me I could keep going when it felt like labor would never end."

"Jenna, I'm not sure Danny needs to know the whole—"

"Oh, you want to hear our college exploits instead?" Jenna asked.

Mike groaned.

"Maybe you could take me through a highlight reel at some point," Daniel said.

"I *definitely* will. Heck, you deserve the extended-length director's cut, for that matter. Today, though, is this one's turn to be the center of attention." She booped her daughter's nose with a pointer finger. "Isn't it, Robbie love? Are you ready to show Uncle Mike your new party trick?"

She set the baby down on her tiny feet, which were encased in a sturdy looking pair of purple sneakers. "You ready to go?"

Robbie gripped one of her mother's fingers in each hand and wobbled.

Mike seemed to sense what was coming and crouched, holding out his arms.

Jenna slipped her fingers out of the baby's fists. Robbie planted one foot on the ground, then another and another before swaying and tumbling into Mike's outstretched hands with a "Ma!"

"You did it!" Mike crowed, scooping the child up and standing. He swayed in a circle, cooing, "You are so strong. Yes, you are."

The baby squealed and patted Mike's chest with two pudgy hands.

Nudging Daniel with an elbow, Jenna whispered, "He's a keeper, see?"

Daniel had no doubt she had a master plan to talk up her friend, what with pointing out how much of a support he was. And normally seeing a man's softer side would draw Daniel in even further.

It *did* draw him in. He liked a man who had layers, and he downright envied how close Mike was to the people he loved. Would that closeness make it impossible to have a relationship with Daniel? An hour-and-a-half drive each way was more than long distance with how tightly Mike was tied to the people in his life.

"Will you be here this weekend, Danny?" Jenna said, jarring him from his worries.

"Daniel." *Oh, hell.* The habitual correction had slipped out. If only he could claw it back.

Mike's eyes widened.

Jenna cocked her head.

"I usually go by Daniel," he said.

"All right, then. *Daniel*," Jenna said, "will you be here this weekend?"

He lifted a shoulder. "Possibly. Depends on my truck."

"Right." Jenna winked. "Mike was telling me how much he's hoping it takes Chuck *days* to get the part in."

Mike groaned. "Jenna."

Daniel laughed. "The alternator's done, but my brakes need work, too. I'll be here until that's finished."

"Excellent." She grinned and took Robbie back from Mike. "You've answered all my questions. For now."

"Best-friend prerogative?" Daniel asked.

She waggled her brows at Mike. "He's hot *and* smart."

Mike's jaw ticked. "And he's going to drive back to Bronco with faulty brakes if you don't stop."

"No, I don't think he will. Not at all." Winking at Daniel, she said her goodbyes and headed up the stairs.

Digging his fingers into his hair, Mike groaned again.

"She's just doing her job as your best friend," Daniel reassured him.

"She takes it seriously."

"Sounds like you do, too. Birth coaching and everything."

"She needed me," Mike said. "Her husband, Rob, was one of my best friends, too. I couldn't let either of them down after he passed. Still can't. Though she has Diego now—her fiancé—which means a bigger support system."

"Seems like 'support system' could be the town's motto."

"Tough times call for tougher people."

Daniel nodded. "And for good people. It shows."

Mike's mouth turned down. "Why didn't you correct me when I first started calling you Danny?"

"I like it, coming from you." More and more, it felt like a pet name.

"You should have said something," Mike said.

"I *like* it." He snagged Mike's hand and squeezed. "It's special."

"But it's your name. Was it part of you trying to hide who you are?"

"Not really," Daniel said. "'Danny' fit better here."

Mike's expression shifted between suspicious and nervous. "And you want to fit into Tenacity because…"

Crap, he needed to be careful with this. He took a deep breath before saying, "Because *you* fit here. And I… I want to see if there's a chance I can fit with you."

Chapter Twelve

Hope battled with doubt in Mike's chest. Danny wanted to see if he fit in Tenacity?

With me?

It was intriguing and tempting and *fast.*

Mike's brain swam, like he was staring at an unfinished jigsaw puzzle on a table, unsure if he had all the pieces to form a whole picture.

He'd been prepared for a few days of getting to know each other. Danny had specifically called his time here an *interlude.* Fitting together—that was a whole other level. Throwing himself into a relationship in the past had only ever ended in devastation—how could he trust that this time, his judgment was sound?

Nor was it only his heart at risk. Finding the room to make space for anyone, let alone someone who came from an entirely different world, would cost the people he loved, too. How could he take time and days away from Cody or from the ranch? Or cut down his hours behind the bar but not have as much money to close the ranch's gap between red and black?

Danny was silent, clearly waiting for Mike to say something.

Unable to make sense of his confusion, Mike latched on to something concrete. "Your brakes, huh?"

"They *do* need to be fixed." Something downright calculated, but somehow also playful, tugged at Danny's mouth.

Mike narrowed his eyes. "Immediately?"

"What if it was more 'out of an abundance of caution'?"

"Because you're a cautious guy?"

"I usually am." Danny shook his head. "But I'm willing to take a risk here, if you are."

"On your...truck repairs?"

"No, Mike, on you," Danny said. "My truck could wait. I can even drive it while I'm waiting for Chuck to get the right pads in. But I can't imagine being given a better chance to spend time with you, so I took it." He sobered. "Provided you want something similar."

"I'm flattered."

Danny winced. "You're flattered, *but*..."

"No." Mike took a step closer. "I'm flattered, *and*."

"And what?"

"And I think you might have a screw loose if you think Tenacity's going to live up to your Bronco Heights expectations, but I'm game to spend time with you while you do."

Danny arched a brow. "Bronco Heights expectations?"

"As if your day-to-day isn't upscale. Letting me call you Danny isn't the only way you've tried to fly under the radar. I'm betting if I went and rooted around in your hotel room, I'd find a monogrammed shaving kit and designer silk pajama pants. And you can't tell me you're using the hotel's shampoo. Your hair smells way too good." Like his mother's herb garden after she went through it with scissors, all rosemary and mint and—

"Hey." Danny threaded a hand through Mike's, a tangible anchor amid all the *what if*s. "Anytime you want to come snoop through my hotel room, it's yours. My suitcase, my toiletry bag that may or may not have my initials on it—" Danny lifted his eyebrows playfully "—and the bed with the rather firm mattress and two-hundred-thread count sheets."

"See? The fact you can recognize how refined the bedding is…"

"It's easy to tell, given I don't wear pajamas."

Mike groaned.

His heart might be urging him to be cautious, but other parts of him were *not*. He'd stolen enough small moments with Danny to want more—their kiss at the rodeo and out in the field, brief moments in the barn and hell, the dance they'd just shared. It all lit him from the inside out. He was impatient to explore what came next.

So long as I keep it something small.

Simple enough that it didn't disrupt his promises to Cody and his parents.

Real enough to try out that chance of *fitting together* that Danny wanted.

Not just Danny. I might want it, too.

Even though he'd always chosen the wrong matches in the past.

"Is your truck in good enough shape to drive out to my place?" he asked.

Goodbye, any chance of waking up rested tomorrow. His schedule only left the hours after Cody fell asleep. With his early mornings, Mike headed for bed not long after his nephew—on the days he wasn't up late serving drinks.

Worth every yawn, though.

"It could for sure make it," Danny said. "If you wanted it to."

I think I do. Whether he was setting himself up for another round of heartache remained to be seen. But as much as Danny's wealth and magnetism was similar to Mike's ex, his kind soul and moments of being down-to-earth were entirely the opposite. Maybe that would be enough. At least to try. "Do you want to come watch a movie or something?"

"When?" Danny asked, happiness twitching at the corners of his mouth.

"Tonight," Mike said. "Cody could sleep through a meteorite strike."

"Name a time, and I will be there."

At 8:23, Mike was racing around his kitchen, trying to get all the dishes into the dishwasher and Cody's daily detritus set to the side. *Seven minutes to go.* He wasn't planning on entertaining in the space, but the layout was open enough to offer a full view of the kitchen and dining nook from the family room, so he wanted it tidy.

Danny probably had a regular housecleaner to make sure his place was spotless.

Ignoring the unsettled state of his stomach, Mike took his inadequacy out on wiping a streak of spaghetti sauce off the counter next to the stove.

One of the stairs on the flight to the second floor creaked.

"Uncle Mike?"

Mike managed to keep his groan inside but not by much. His nephew's hopeful little tone suggested the boy wasn't suffering from a tummy bug or a fever. This was stalling extraordinaire.

"Yeah, Cody?"

"I'm thirsty."

Tactic number one. Well, at least Mike could solve thirst in less than five minutes. "Where's your glass of water, bud?"

"I finished it." Cody shuffled into the kitchen. He was wearing the Marvel-print pajamas Ellen had given him for Christmas last year, along with a pair of plush dinosaur slippers that looked more *Flintstones cartoon* than *authentic T. rex.* He held out his empty glass.

Mike pointed a dirty plate in the direction of the fridge before slotting the dish into the bottom rack.

"I'm hungry, too," his nephew announced.

And there's number two.

And as much as Mike was desperate to get his nephew to bed, Cody being a growing eight-year-old meant it wasn't unusual for him to claim he needed a snack at bedtime.

"Toast with peanut butter, or peanut butter with toast?" he joked, getting the last few dishes into the rack and closing the door.

"What about popcorn?" Cody's gaze flicked hungrily to the bowl on the counter, still empty but set up under the air popper.

"Oh, *that's* your game, is it?" Mike said. He didn't blame his nephew, though the what-I-really-want-is-snacks angle was going to threaten Mike's overarching aim—uninterrupted time with Danny.

Ever since their moment in the tack room yesterday, it was all he could think of. The few minutes they'd been alone at the club this afternoon had ramped up his need to be alone with the smart, sexy cowboy.

Taking a seat at the table, Cody looked more impish than apologetic.

"Popcorn is not on the menu, my friend. Your options are toast or no toast," Mike said. "And while you're waiting, you can get all the yarn cleaned up." Cody had learned how to braid embroidery floss at school yesterday. True to his usual tendency to latch on to anything novel, he was now on a tear to turn anything he could into a friendship bracelet.

Three colorful bands circled Mike's wrist, proof of his nephew's tongue-between-the-teeth, finger-chapped efforts.

"O-*kay*, Uncle Mike."

At least he was in a good mood. And hopefully Danny would tolerate having company for the first few minutes of their date.

Mike was pushing down the lever on the toaster when a sharp knock sounded on the door.

Cody dropped the tangle of yarn he'd collected. "I'll get it."

"No, you won't," Mike said gently, motioning for Cody to keep tidying before striding through the living area to answer.

Danny stood a foot back from the doormat. He clutched a mixed bouquet of flowers in one hand and a bottle of wine in the other.

Wanting to explain about Cody being up without the boy in question hearing, Mike scooted out the door and closed it behind him.

"Hey," he said, taking advantage of Danny's full hands to cup the other man's cheeks and greet him with a tender kiss.

"Mmm." Danny deepened the kiss, ringing his arms around Mike's back despite bearing gifts. The bottle rested against Mike's spine and the florist's paper tickled the back of his neck. "Hey, yourself."

"I have to explain. I—"

Danny's expression fell into disappointment.

"Oh, no, it's nothing bad," Mike said. "But Cody's not *quite* asleep."

"And you want me to take off?" His guest's voice was uncharacteristically tentative.

"No! Not at all. Unless you don't want to be here… But he shouldn't be up much longer. He'll have his snack and then go back upstairs. And hopefully conk out quick."

"Mike." Danny passed him the flowers and rested his now-free hand on Mike's hip. His deft fingers flexed, and he shifted forward the last couple inches, bringing their bodies together. "I very much still want to be here."

Mike swallowed. "Good."

Danny lifted a brow. "Can I come in now?"

"Oh! Yes. Of course. I just wanted to explain—without an audience."

"I get it."

Stepping back, Mike stared at the bouquet he'd been given.

"You brought me flowers. Can't say anyone's thought to do that before."

The porch light caught a hint of color rising on Danny's face. "Any house looks more cheerful with flowers on the table. I'd put them in water soon, though. I've been hanging on to them for a few hours."

"Of course!" God, he was acting like he was in a fog.

Mainly because, triangulated somewhere in the middle of the kiss and the closeness and the heat in Danny's eyes, Mike *was* in a fog.

It would sure be nice if he could at least *pretend* to be level.

He opened the door and held it open for his date, motioning with the flowers for Danny to enter.

A bouncing Cody mobbed them the second they were through the frame. "Danny! Hi! Do you want to see my room? I've been making friendship bracelets. I should make you one, though Uncle Mike told me to clean it all up. Probably so you won't think we live like slobs. Grandma says we are sometimes. Uncle Mike, the toast is done." He narrowed his eyes at Mike. "Your hair is all messy. But I saw you put stuff in it. And you were in the bathroom forever. Like, a half an *hour.*"

"Bud," Mike said, putting his nephew in a headlock and giving him a knuckle rub in hopes of distracting him enough to get him to shut up, "Danny doesn't need a blow-by-blow of our life. Let's go deal with the peanut butter."

He didn't have a vase, so he pulled out a plastic water jug and put the flowers in it. He turned his attention to the broad-shouldered, classy man in the middle of toeing out of his shoes.

"If you brought the wine for us, I could pour us each a glass."

"Save it, open it—your choice," Danny said.

Mike studied the label. "Can't say I get a lot of wine experience at the club, other than house red and house white. Does pinot noir pair with popcorn?"

"Anything pairs with popcorn."

"I really want popcorn more than peanut butter toast," Cody interjected.

And I really want to be done parenting for the day.

"Tell you what," Mike said, shuffling the boy into the kitchen. "I'll make you some and put it in your lunch tomorrow. You can have it at recess."

"Yes." Cody pumped his fist. "You know…maybe I'm not hungry after all."

Of-freaking-course. Mike closed his eyes and counted to five. "Cody…"

Small arms wrapped around his waist. "I love you."

Nothing like Cody's embrace to remind him of his priorities.

"I love you, too." He dropped a kiss onto his nephew's head. "Want me to come tuck you in again?"

Cody nodded.

"Give me a couple of minutes," Mike said to Danny, motioning to the couch on the other side of the half wall separating the kitchen from the living area. "Please, make yourself comfortable."

He got Cody into bed as fast as he could without making it obvious to his nephew how much he was rushing.

When he got back downstairs, Danny was pouring popcorn kernels into the well of the air popper. Two glasses of ruby-red wine sat on the kitchen table, next to the pile of yarn his nephew had dropped and forgotten for a second time.

Mike blinked, unable to rip his gaze off Danny's forearms. He must have rolled up his sleeves while Mike had been out of the room, because holy hell, if all that muscular perfection had been exposed when he'd arrived, Mike would have noticed in two seconds. It seemed to be the way Danny preferred to wear his shirts, and exactly no parts of Mike were upset about that.

Danny came over and reached for one of Mike's hands.

When they threaded their fingers together, a good half of Mike's nerves settled.

The other half jumped, anticipating the real reason he'd invited his date to his house.

"Will Cody take long to go to sleep?" Danny asked.

"Hard to say. It's unusual for me to have anyone over on a school night, so he was excited, even though I'd emphasized he'd be in bed by the time you arrived."

He let his gaze drift along Danny's white button-up shirt, tucked into a pair of flat-fronted dress pants made of some fine wool blend. Not quite popcorn-and-a-movie clothes.

"You dressed up," Mike said.

Danny's thumb brushed a line on the inside of Mike's wrist. A light touch, but it cascaded from his wrist to the center of his chest and beyond. A steady heat settled low in his belly. He spread his fingers on Danny's hip, hooking his own thumb through a belt loop. The man was all lean muscle. The fabric of Danny's pants was thinner than the jeans he'd had on when they'd gotten close out in the barn. Mike let his hand skim around to the curve where a palm on the waist became a far more intimate touch, questing for a hint of something they'd have to leave the kitchen to find.

"Shockingly, the Tenacity Inn doesn't offer laundry service." Danny's observation was in a light enough tone to not be a dig. "So until I hit up the laundromat tomorrow, you're getting office attire."

Mike was not complaining. He'd enjoyed the man in denim and work shirts, but seeing him in something more suited for a boardroom than a barn was a hell of a turn-on.

"You could have used my washer and dryer," he offered.

"Mmm, yeah, sexy, doing laundry together," Danny teased.

"True, but it's about on par with my life right now. I cannot believe how much laundry eight-year-old boys generate."

"It's always something, I bet," Danny said.

"Yeah." Mike rubbed the back of his neck, hoping his simple T-shirt was a nice enough choice. He might have spent extra time on his hair, as his nephew had so kindly exposed, but he hadn't put on anything fancier than usual. "It won't be forever. Maggie will be home before Christmas. But for now…"

"For now, it's more important than anything," Danny said.

Mike's throat tightened. "Yeah."

"How about for tonight you pretend the only needs on your to-do list are your own?"

Oh god. Yes, please.

"Tell you a secret?" Mike said. His voice was thicker than he'd like, but swallowing wasn't doing a thing.

A hint of cologne drifted in, woodsy and warm, as Danny leaned close. "I'm intrigued."

"Well, I don't want to oversell on 'secret' here. It might be obvious."

Danny hooked one of Mike's belt loops and pulled him closer. "Tell me."

"The main thing I need right now…is you."

"Mike." A low noise rumbled at the back of Danny's throat. Not a growl, exactly. But not *not* a growl.

Satisfaction filled Mike—damn, it was good to know he wasn't alone on the edge.

"Yeah?" he said.

"You're going to have to explain how you want to go about this," Danny said. "I don't want to make a mistake, being we're not alone in the house."

"As far as Cody knows, we're watching a movie." Mike slid his hands up Danny's back. Their chests pressed together, heat singeing through their shirts. Tilting his chin up the fraction he needed to kiss the taller man, he said, "But he'll be asleep any minute, and if we get sidetracked after it's over, well…"

"I am—" lips teased his, the barest of kisses "—distractible."

Before there was time to reply, Danny drove his fingers into Mike's hair and took the kiss from featherlight to falling-off-a-cliff deep. Good God. What this man could do with his mouth. Mike shivered, tracing the tip of his tongue along Danny's lower lip. A silent entreaty met with a stroke of Danny's own tongue.

Was it possible to melt together with someone? Until the edges of himself and the edges of the man in his arms blurred into something indistinguishable?

He tore his mouth away, almost panting for air.

"I'm—" Dang, he sounded like a creaking signpost. He cleared his throat. "You're not the only distractible one here. And we might want to wait a few minutes before we lose our heads."

Danny's gaze was molten. Parted lips, breath hot on Mike's cheek. "Yeah, of course. I mean, popcorn and a movie can totally live up to the way you kiss."

Mike choked out a laugh at the sarcasm. "With any luck, my nephew will fall asleep faster than he ever has in his life."

They grabbed the popcorn, ferried the wine to the coffee table and settled into the couch, side by side with a few inches between them. Mike pulled up the menu on his streaming service and pointed out a few suspense movies he'd been meaning to watch.

The second Danny's fingers nudged against his in the popcorn bowl, he lost all semblance of caring what choice they settled on.

Danny lifted his brows, a hint of suggestion. "Something new? The most recent *Mission: Impossible*, maybe? Or a classic? Looks like they have *The Talented Mr. Ripley*. I don't know if any character has ever been as hot as that depiction of Dickie Greenleaf."

"I haven't seen it."

An exaggerated gasp filled the air, and Danny threw a piece

of popcorn at Mike's cheek. "I'm deciding for us. Turn it on. If you hate it, we can—well, no. If you hate it, you have to pretend to love it. I didn't truly know I was gay until I watched this movie."

Mike teased the hair at Danny's wrist with his fingertips. "Are you serious?"

"No." He cracked a smile. "Well, maybe a little. It has *sexual awakening* all over it—trust me."

Not something I need to worry about when I'm around you.

However, he was game for the choice.

They fell into the color-saturated world of coastal Italy, enjoying the building suspense and munching on the bowl of popcorn until only kernels and a few streaks of salt-flecked butter remained. Mike reached forward to put the bowl on the table.

As he sat back, Danny shifted closer until their shoulders brushed. Curious fingers stroked Mike's knee.

Yes, please.

Mike picked up Danny's hand and brought it to his lips, slowly kissing each knuckle. The warmth of his date's skin was a magnet, pulling Mike in. Bringing his legs up, he angled one bent knee over the built thigh next to his and braced his other foot on the coffee table for balance. With Danny's hand still clutched in his and resting against his chest, he glanced left, hoping for some sort of sign that all his shifting and minor acrobatics were welcome.

A hooded, brown gaze met his silent query. Danny rested his free hand on Mike's knee and swept his thumb back and forth.

Good enough.

Danny tugged his hand free and circled his arm around Mike's shoulders. "Comfortable?"

The question brushed across the sensitive skin behind Mike's ear.

He nodded.

Mike didn't know what to do with his hands. Danny was getting to touch him, but with the way they were tangled together, there wasn't an easy way for Mike to tease his fingers along any of the slivers of skin exposed to him.

"Liking the movie?" Danny asked.

He hummed in confirmation. It was fun to watch something different from his usual comedies and superhero flicks. He'd be even more into the film were he anywhere else but wrapped up in Danny. Their tender embrace made it hard to focus on the plot. His body was lighting up in all the places where it currently touched Danny's. He didn't need to be turned on by actors right now. The only person Mike needed was settled into his couch, stroking a mesmerizing pattern on his shoulder and his knee.

Danny's hand dragged up Mike's thigh.

Yes, please, that direction—

He skimmed right past Mike's zippered fly and palmed his stomach over his shirt, then up to splay wide between his pecs.

"Your heart is racing," Danny rasped.

"No kidding."

Mike's eyes fluttered shut, and he let go a little more, easing into the all-encompassing hold of the arm behind his back and the weight of the tender touch on his chest. He let his head fall back against the couch.

Lips nuzzled his exposed skin. Nips and licks, a scrape of teeth along his thrumming pulse. Soft hair tickled the underside of his chin, and a shuddery breath escaped him. Need pulled at his groin. He was seconds away from being painfully hard.

The music changed onscreen with a blast of jazz on the speakers, and Mike startled.

Danny drew back, expression questioning.

"I know you love this movie, but ever since you started

touching me, I can't even keep track of the characters' names," Mike confessed.

"Mmm." Danny crept his hand south. "Forget the characters' names—I want to make you forget your *own*."

"Keep touching me, and I will."

Not here, though. Damn, how were they going to make this work?

Chapter Thirteen

Mike slid out of Daniel's embrace and stumbled to his feet, sending a wave of doubt through Daniel.

"Did I do something wrong?" he asked.

Shaking his head, Mike chuckled in disbelief.

"You didn't have to get up. I'd give you space, if you want," Daniel offered.

It was like his body was negatively charged now that Mike had put distance between them. He yearned to have the willing weight against his body again.

"No." Mike's refusal pitched toward panic. "We are not stopping this time. Not unless you want to."

"I figured having my hands on you was a clear sign of what I want."

"Yes. *Yes*." A long breath gusted from Mike's lungs. "We can't here, though."

Easing off the couch, Daniel closed the gap until he could feel the heat of Mike's body through his clothes again. "Tell me where you want me, then."

"In my bed, Danny."

Pleasure trailed along his hips as Mike slid his fingers to the leather belt Daniel had waffled over wearing. A trail of kisses traced along the open collar of his shirt. Rough fingers flicked open a button, then another, the rasp of calluses belying the gentle touch.

A rush of anticipation washed down Daniel's limbs. "That's an irresistible invitation."

Mike's cheeks turned an adorable shade of pink.

"*You're* impossible to resist," Daniel added.

God, he'd waited a long time to feel this excited about spending a night with someone.

Throat bobbing, Mike backed up. "Okay. Let me… I'll be right back."

He sped away, making almost no noise as he jogged up the stairs.

Pulse galloping, Daniel strained for the sound of a small voice or childlike complaint. There was nothing but the click of a door before the object of his fantasies reappeared, his face filled with hope and hot intent.

Mike crooked a finger, stepping backward in the direction of a short hallway with two doors and a closet. Stopping with his back to one of the doors, he held one hand out to Daniel and palmed the knob with his other. Anticipation crept from his soft, sensual mouth into his eyes, lighting the gold with tempting heat.

"It's nothing fancy," he said, closing and locking the door after they'd entered.

"You say that as if I'll notice anything about the room other than you being in it."

The pale gray paint on the walls blurred behind the rustic wood of the dresser and the posts of the four-poster bed as Daniel prowled forward, his hands in Mike's soft hair and his lips capturing the salty sweet hints of popcorn and wine.

They landed on the bed. Daniel's back pressed into the soft mattress. Hard, work-wrought muscles sprawled across his body. Flat abs against his side, a taut thigh angled over his own. Mike's hot gaze sizzled across Daniel's skin. A hand tugged at the rest of his shirt buttons, then at the tails tucked into his pants. He untangled his hands from the soft, tousled curls falling across Mike's forehead and stripped the younger man of his shirt.

Time to deal with the necessities before they got any further. "I'm negative, tested recently. You?"

"Tested negative in the fall." Mike's short breaths clipped his words. "Haven't been with anyone since."

Daniel pulled a trio of condoms and a travel packet of lube from his pocket and tossed it all onto the nightstand. "If we need them. No expectations, though."

"You might not have any expectations," Mike said. "I sure do."

"Yeah?"

"Hell yes. Have you seen you? And you're in my bed, and I'm pretty sure I'm the luckiest man in the world right now."

The total lack of artifice sliced right through Daniel's guard. Groaning, he shook his head.

Two hands seemed an unfair limitation when presented with a body like Mike's to explore.

The dim light of the room shone golden across muscled pecs.

Daniel traced his fingers across smooth skin. This man deserved reverence, softness, the utmost care. He traced his way down the lightly furred trail to where skin-warmed denim and the cold metal of a belt buckle covered a bulge he wanted to explore more than anything.

Hands shaking with the thirst pouring through his veins, he fumbled with the buckle. He drew down the zipper, dragging two fingers along the rock-hard, cotton-covered ridge below. Gasping, Mike gripped Daniel's shoulder with a callused hand. His golden gaze begged for Daniel to follow through on the silent promise that he'd made in undoing Mike's jeans.

Why rush, though? This could end up being a rare moment in time, or at least one they would have to be patient before they could relive again. And if Daniel knew one thing—Mike Cooper was worth being infinitely patient.

Stretched out on his simple comforter, Mike was a work of art. All young vitality and beautiful heart. Daniel scooted his hand up from Mike's fly, resting it on the hard space between his navel and waistband. He leaned in for what he meant to be a gentle kiss. He wanted Mike to know how much he was treasuring this moment, the willingness to let Daniel into his life.

Did Daniel want more? Did he want to be in Mike's heart, too? *Of course.* He'd be a fool not to want whatever he was able to find with Mike.

But in the absence of certainty, Daniel could show him how much he valued the younger man taking a risk on him.

Mike's mouth demolished Daniel's intended gentleness with a fervor that took him out at the knees. Goddamn, the man could kiss. Daniel met the passionate touch with his own need, tasting Mike back, betraying his slipping control.

Their chests pressed together, the tantalizing slide of skin on skin. Daniel skimmed his palms under Mike's pants and underwear, over the smooth curve of his ass. It was impossible not to grip, to pull his hips forward.

The tease of fabric over arousal was almost too much to handle. If Daniel didn't get a hold of himself, he was going to come far before he wanted to. Taking a grounding breath, he forced his pulse to settle. The tension settled just enough to make it bearable.

Nipping at Daniel's lower lip, groaning deep in his throat, Mike was a blur of desperate kisses and frantic hands. Daniel's pants were at his thighs, his erection straining in Mike's hand. Jangling desire flashed in jagged colors, coursing through Daniel's brain with every slow stroke of that rough grip.

Mike struggled to shove down his own pants. Chuckling, Daniel took over, sliding cotton over angled hips until Mike's erection sprang free.

Loosening his grip, Mike looped his thumb around himself and tucked his arousal against Daniel's.

Oh, *God.* Daniel moaned. So damn good. He swore into Mike's shoulder.

"How do you want—" Mike's thumb stroked the underside of Daniel's crown.

"Like *that.*"

"Mmm, I like you losing control."

Another swipe of Mike's thumb, and Daniel was swearing more.

A chuckle rumbled from Mike. "Didn't know it would be so easy to wind you up."

"I've been in knots from the moment I first saw you at the club," Daniel admitted.

Damn, should he have said that?

Honesty was one thing.

Laying everything out, the reality of being in pieces for this man, might not be so smart.

Mike's hand stilled, and he pressed a hint of a kiss to the corner of Daniel's mouth before trailing over to his ear. "Months ago?"

"Yeah."

"Me, too."

"It's been the best torment," Daniel murmured. An endless well of want throbbed, empty at his core. Having his erection in Mike's hand, against Mike's arousal without moving was going to kill him.

Hell of a way to go, mind you. But still. Self-preservation demanded another slick thrust.

"Would you top me?" The request flooded from Mike.

Daniel was glad for the clarity, and even gladder that it lined up with his own preferences.

"My pleasure, sweetheart," he said. Nothing to be done about the rough gravel in his voice at this point, so he rolled with it. He was going to get to be inside this man. No point in being shy about how much the prospect affected him.

Daniel rolled with Mike, settling between his legs and sifting shaking fingers through his hair while tasting his mouth like he was a decadent treat.

Mike clutched Daniel's back, ten points of desperation on slick skin. He whimpered—*whimpered*—against Daniel's lips.

The vulnerability pulled a moan from Daniel's own throat. He rocked against Mike, mimicking how close he wanted to be, *planned* to be, as soon as he ensured his lover was prepared.

"Please."

Mike was begging.

Daniel was helpless.

"Christ, I'm lost for you," he confessed.

"*Daniel. Please.*"

"Okay. I've got you. I promise."

After shucking his pants and underwear with zero ceremony, he was infinitely more careful with Mike's, sliding them down his legs and reveling in all the hair-sprinkled skin and the kind of thighs a man got when he was on the back of a horse for hours every day.

Mike was up on his elbows, serving a look liable to burn Daniel to a cinder. He probably wanted Daniel to come in for a kiss, but Daniel was more interested in the length he'd just revealed.

He eased down the bed, tasting and testing all the way down. Nibbles along Mike's stomach and inner thighs earned gasps. A lick at his base had him white knuckling the sheet.

Daniel wasn't sure he'd ever been smiling so widely right before wrapping his lips around an erection, but all he knew was Mike made him happy, and he wanted to do the same in return.

Mike released the sheet and threaded his fingers into Daniel's hair, gripping just enough to hold on without pulling.

"You don't have to," Mike said.

"Mmm, but I do. I want to make sure you're ready."

"Okay…" Mike patted a wild hand along the nightstand and thrust the packets down the bed.

Daniel tore into the lube and slicked his fingers. He started prepping Mike with a finger while kissing and laving his thick crown.

Mike cursed and arched his hips. Daniel pressed his own hips into the bed, desperate for release.

He couldn't. Not before he got to experience the guaranteed perfection of falling apart with Mike Cooper.

Within a couple of minutes, Mike was a writhing mess on the bed. Danny kissed and coaxed, the singular devotion turning Mike into fire.

"Stop, stop," he said, hardly able to breathe from the pleasure.

Danny did, drawing back on his haunches, face flushed and gaze heavy lidded. "Everything okay?"

Okay? *Okay?* Mike almost laughed. "More than. But I want to finish *with* you."

Danny prowled forward.

Mike went to roll over—a habit from last summer—but Danny held him in place with a palm to the chest.

"What about this way?" Danny asked.

Oh. He'd never tried having sex face-to-face. But…how would it feel to get lost in those dark brown depths? He nodded.

Being covered like this was different. Immersed in Danny, dwelling in his care and deliberate touches. They kissed, a languid moment in time where desperation sizzled in Mike's veins.

These first moments, first touches were so damn precious.

And as much as Danny was guarded, he wasn't shying

away from being close to Mike. Each shift of fingers and lips suggested Danny was experiencing similar sensory overload.

It was like being warmed by the sun until Mike was pliable, ready to be molded to Danny's every desire.

A tilt of Danny's hips, a hard nudge…then the glorious pressure of a beautiful man sliding into his entrance. Just an inch and a pause.

A wave washed over Mike, pleasure mixed with the tight stretch.

"Tell me when you're ready for more." Danny murmured the quiet words along Mike's jaw.

Oh God, this man and his words and his intent… Mike was in pieces, and Danny's endless brown gaze was the safest place to put himself back together.

The tension eased, and his body craved more, the rush of being as close as they could possibly get.

"More. *Everything.* You feel so good."

Danny followed through, driving Mike to the brink with a slow, tantalizing thrust. He was breathing hard. His forehead pressed to Mike's shoulder.

With their hips flush—

—*it's going to wreck me.*

"Faster," Mike urged, shifting under that hard body, trying to get to the promise he could just feel the edges of. He needed to get to the center of it, the all-encompassing meld he craved.

"Nah." Danny's smirk was infuriatingly beautiful. Another slow stroke had Mike losing control, writhing under the other man's touch. "These moments might be hard to come by. I plan to memorize each second."

Need clawed in Mike's belly, on the verge of agony. Being held, caressed, *loved* should've felt indulgent, euphoric.

It was so goddamned petrifying.

"How are you so in control?" Mike rasped.

"Why—" dark eyes latched on to him, all pupil except for

a thin rim of rich brown "—do you think—" a thrust, a scrape of teeth on Mike's throat "—I'm in control?"

"I'm going to fall apart if we don't speed up, and you seem so together."

Danny's breathy *ha* was all disbelief. "I'm in tatters, though. Good thing you pull me together."

Oh. *Oh.*

Danny was…

Holy hell.

Mike was lost to the build of each sweet slide. His erection was close to oversensitive, caught between his own abs and the trimmed hair on Danny's hard stomach. Trying to hold in the bliss for as long as he could, Mike clung to Danny's back and met each flex until his world fractured around him. Pleasure crashed along his skin, over and under and through, like surf hammering a beach, changing the shape of the sand, never to be the same again. And Danny followed.

Danny braced on his elbows above Mike, taking heaving breaths and wearing a stunned expression. "Wow."

"Yeah," Mike breathed. "That was…"

"Not 'that.' *You.* You're incredible." A line of kisses emphasized the sweet declaration.

Mike wasn't sure he'd ever felt so satiated. Looping his weak arms around Danny, he gave himself a minute to calm down.

His lover didn't seem to be in a rush to move.

Eventually, though, Danny laid a tender kiss on Mike's mouth before making sure the condom was in place.

"Give me a minute—I'll get you a cloth." He slid away, then went to the bathroom to clean up.

Mike burrowed under the covers, hoping Danny wouldn't rush off right away. They hadn't discussed how their night would end.

Damn, he didn't want it to—not yet.

After a couple of minutes, Danny came back to bed, carrying a warm, damp cloth. He snuggled in next to Mike, taking care of him, wrapping him in comfort. The world felt lighter when Mike was in Danny's arms.

Chapter Fourteen

"Hey, Mike." The quiet voice drifted into the shadows of sleep.

Mike roused, cracking open an eye, smiling at the sight of rumpled dark hair and a strong shoulder serving as the perfect pillow.

"I fell asleep," he said. "Did you?"

"No," Danny murmured.

"How long did you let me sleep for?"

"Long enough that I think I've memorized how it feels to hold you."

Oh god, the guy knew what to say to make a person melt.

"I should go, though," Danny continued, his words a clear apology. A sated, almost woozy smile followed.

"It's taking all of my better angels not to invite you to stay."

"I understand why you can't. You have more to think about than just you and me. It could confuse Cody if he woke up and I was sitting at your kitchen table."

"Yeah, probably."

We might get there, though.

It was too easy to picture falling for this man.

He reluctantly peeled himself away from Danny's warmth and tugged on his jeans while the other man got dressed.

Once ready, they crept down the hall and through the living room.

Mike glanced at the clock on the mantel. "Oh, ouch."

"Not keeping rancher's hours," Daniel said as he slipped into his shoes and jacket, seemingly trying not to make a sound.

Mike followed him onto the porch.

"You're going to be a zombie tomorrow," Danny said, tracing a hand along Mike's jaw.

"It's worth it."

"Might be your orgasm talking." Hungry lips stole another kiss.

"Oh, it's definitely that." And in his post-sex haze, an idea surfaced. "Don't leave on Friday. Stay for the weekend."

Danny stilled.

Mike cringed at his lack of chill. What was he thinking? Danny had already delayed his departure more than once.

"Sorry. Forgot about your out-of-state meetings for a second, there. Brain's fuzzy," he said, scrambling for anything that would make him sound less needy.

"My meetings might be up in the air," Danny said cautiously.

"They are?" Hope leaped in Mike's chest. "I don't want to ask you to shell out more to stay here, but there is Friday-night trivia at the Social Club this week…"

"I can afford another night," Danny said.

"Doesn't mean it's fair to ask you to. Money still matters, even if you have a lot of it."

He couldn't shake the feeling that money mattered *because* Danny had a lot of it. The man seemed to be enjoying living in Mike's world on a temporary basis, but how long could this go on for before Danny tired of the slower, simpler life Tenacity had to offer?

Danny blew out a breath, hard enough to make his lips puff. "Will you be bartending during trivia?"

Mike shook his head. "Night off. And Cody's sleeping over

at my parents'. Jenna demands victory and wants me for all the fun facts I've memorized thanks to my encyclopedia of a nephew."

"I'll see what I can do." Danny stole one last kiss. "You should get to bed. You're going to blink and it will be five o'clock. Don't fall off your horse in the morning."

Mike suspected he'd never get tired of tasting those lips, which was about to become a damn problem. "How about you join Cody and me for our Thursday-afternoon pie at the Silver Spur Café, and you can make sure I safely kept my seat?"

What. The. Hell.

He needed *not* to have conversations after midnight. He'd lasso the invite back in if he could. Throwing it out right after asking about trivia night? Talk about oozing desperation.

"I am in for pie," Danny said. "Any minute you have free, I'm up for sharing."

Another fleeting kiss, a sheepish smile, and then Danny was walking away from the porch, tossing his keys into the air and catching them every few steps.

Mike stepped back and slumped against the door, his thin T-shirt letting through the chill off the wood.

With the energy still snapping in his veins, sleep was going to be a long time coming.

"Your usual, Michael?" asked Barb, one of the long-standing waitresses at the Silver Spur Café. She was a decade or so younger than Mike's mom but was friends with her through the Tenacity quilting circle and fussed over Mike and Cody accordingly.

Her pen, plucked out of her gray-streaked copper bun, hovered over her notepad. Cody and Mike shared a bench of their usual booth in the front corner of the homey café. Mike had taken the aisle seat. His nephew was busy examining the plasticized menu as if he hadn't been looking at it weekly since before he'd learned how to read.

Mike shook his head. "Give us a few minutes, please, Barb. We're waiting for a guest."

Curiosity lit her sharp, pale features. "Someone I know?"

"Probably not," Mike said, following up with a yawn.

"Cup of English Breakfast while you wait?"

"Yeah, thanks." He pressed the heels of his hands to his eyelids.

"Do we need to have another conversation about burning the candle at both ends?" she said gently.

He shot her a beleaguered look.

"Or are the shadows under your eyes a one-time thing? Maybe related to your *guest*?"

"Uncle Mike had Danny over last night," Cody offered. "They watched a movie and had popcorn." He affected a pout. "And I had to go to *bed*."

"And did you?" Her eyebrow lifted with the authority of someone who had gone through the gauntlet with her own children.

"Yes," Cody said.

"He did," Mike confirmed.

"The movie had *twelve* swear words," Cody offered, looking quite proud of himself.

Barb stifled a smile. "You could hear it from your bedroom, I take it?"

"I had the door open." He held up his small hand. "I'm allowed a crack this wide."

Thank God Mike had remembered to sneak upstairs and shut it after he and Danny had turned off the movie.

She squeezed Mike's shoulder. "Always with your hands full."

"Keeps me on my toes enough, you'd think I was a ballerina."

The bell over the door dinged, catching Barb's attention. Her jaw dropped.

"Oh, my word," she mumbled. "Have you had your hands full of him, too?"

Mike couldn't blame her for the suggestive joke. It was hard to take his own eyes off Danny as he made his way across the restaurant. He left a trail of intrigue in his wake—raised eyebrows, quiet speculation.

"Michael," Barb breathed. "He is—"

She wisely stopped her comment before Danny got in earshot.

The windswept look worked for him. His cheeks were flushed. He wasn't wearing his Stetson, and his dark hair was tousled. He ran a hand through it as he approached. Then he took off his jacket before sliding into the empty bench seat on the other side of the table, folding the fabric in a careful stack on the vinyl.

"Hey," Mike said, fighting a wave of unwanted shyness.

"Sorry I'm late," Danny said, checking his watch with a wince. "Phone call with my father went long. He's less than impressed with me having truck troubles during branding season. Not that he actually needs me—he's got plenty of hands—but he likes to maintain the illusion created when all his sons pitch in." His gaze flicked to Barb's name tag. "What's your recommendation, Barb? Strawberry rhubarb or lemon meringue?"

"The lemon's my favorite, but then, I like to mix some tartness with my sweets." She blinked, all feigned innocence. "Coffee for you, dear? Or tea? Michael has been yawning since he arrived."

"Unlike Mike, I wasn't up with the sun, and if I have caffeine now, I'll never sleep," Danny said. He caught Mike's eye, tilted his head toward Cody and mouthed, *Milkshake?*

Mike jerked a nod.

Danny smiled at Barb. "Let's get milkshakes—one vanilla, one chocolate—and three glasses. We'll do a taste test."

Barb scribbled on her pad. "Want to do that with the pie, too?"

Mike okayed the idea, and Barb bustled off to deal with their order, pausing to ride herd on the large group of high-school kids who were chowing down on fries and making enough noise to drown out the Carrie Underwood song drifting down from the speakers in the ceiling.

Cody's eyes were still wide with hero worship as he leaned across the table. "We never get milkshakes *and* pie."

Danny winced and sent Mike a silent apology.

"Special occasion," Mike said. "He can climb around in the barn after dinner to shed the extra energy."

"Speaking of dinner," Danny said, "do you have any plans for it before trivia tomorrow?"

A spark he could only describe as victory burned from his belly to his chest. Nerves, too. For some reason, introducing Danny to more of his friends seemed like a bigger deal than it had been to extend the invite to the ranch.

Danny agreed to join Mike for dinner with Jenna, Diego and Diego's sister, Nina, at Castillo's. The small flick of his eyebrow conveyed a subtle, unspoken question: *And after trivia?* It made Mike's pulse skip.

He took a sip of his tea to try to wet his dry mouth. The hot liquid seared his tongue, and he gulped. The burn spread to his throat. He managed to get it down, but his eyes were watering.

"You okay?" Danny said, brows drawn.

"Yeah," Mike croaked. "Forgot it was a fresh cup."

Cody's head tilted. "Think twice, act once, Uncle Mike."

Mike snorted at his own words being turned around on him.

"Guess what," Cody continued, clearly done with adult conversation. "Bianca showed me how to do knots instead of just braiding today." He jammed his hand into his pocket and came out with a closed fist. "It's for you, Danny."

Turning his wrist, Cody revealed an unevenly knotted bracelet of three different shades and thicknesses of blue embroidery thread.

"Oh, cool, Cody. Look at the colors." Danny's surprise was clear. He put on a smile. "You worked so hard on it. Thank you."

"Do you want it on your right wrist or your left?" the boy asked.

Mike held in a groan. "Cody, maybe Danny doesn't—"

"Better tie it tight so it doesn't fall off." Danny held out his left arm toward the offered bracelet.

As Cody knotted the ends together, tongue poking out between his teeth, Mike could feel Danny's kindness tying his heart up equally tight.

Danny rolled one of the knots back and forth with the fingers of his other hand. "I haven't done anything crafty since I went to summer camp. Long enough ago I can almost preface it with 'once upon a time.'"

"I went, too. It was the best. I should talk to Maggie about sending Cody," Mike said.

"Like, to stay overnight?" His nephew's voice had lost all his enthusiasm. He sounded so small.

"Only if you want to," Mike said.

"I always went with a friend," Danny said gently. "We had a great time."

Cody chewed on the inside of his lip and looked up at Mike with trepidation.

A needed reminder that his nephew had been more of a homebody since Maggie left. Mike and his parents were keeping a close eye on Cody, in case his emotions escalated past a healthy level of missing his mom. So far, Cody had been recovering from his sad or nervous moments pretty quickly.

Mike put his arm around the boy and squeezed. "Just a suggestion. And Danny has a good idea—we ask if Payton or Adam could go with you. But if you don't want to, you can be my right-hand man during summer holidays."

"Okay," Cody whispered. His eyes were getting red around the edges. Hopefully the food would arrive soon to distract his sensitive nephew.

Danny studied them both with an unreadable gaze.

"Hey, Cody," their guest broke in, flipping over the kid's paper placemat to the blank side and pulling a pen out of his inside jacket pocket. "Have you ever played super tic-tac-toe?"

Cody shook his head.

Danny sketched one extra-large tic-tac-toe grid, and then added a small grid inside each of the big squares. He explained how the players were trying to win the small, individual grids, and to win them in a way that created three-in-a-row on the big grid to be the ultimate victor. Complicated, but not to the point of making it inaccessible for an eight-year-old.

Mike's insides warmed. Did Danny know how amazing it was that he'd given Cody the benefit of the doubt, recognizing the kid was bright and capable of a challenge?

Even sweeter was how Danny had recognized the need for a subtle distraction and hadn't drawn attention to Cody's sensitive reaction. For someone who'd claimed not to spend a lot of time with children, Danny certainly had good instincts with Mike's nephew.

Oh, man. It was way too easy to picture sharing more of these small moments. The two of them could take Cody for a trail ride, or for a day trip to the dinosaur museum just over the North Dakota border. Double-header movie nights together, where they watched something family friendly first, and then sent Cody to bed and enjoyed something more adult, some more time alone.

Mike's chest tightened. Could he trust that vision? Nothing

about him and Danny made sense on paper. And letting his mind run free with sweet possibilities guaranteed more pain when the inevitable end arrived.

The competitors started marking Xs and Os into the grid. Cody's tongue was screwed up in the corner of his mouth, which made for a rare stretch of silence as he focused. Danny, on the other hand, seemed to be able to talk and play at the same time, so Mike used the few uninterrupted minutes to tease out some of the basic Danny-related information he hadn't yet managed to pry from the man. Apparently Danny had never met a plate of nachos he could say no to (the hotter the salsa, the better), he tried to get away somewhere tropical every year to go snorkeling and the most mind-boggling thing he'd seen in his life were the northern lights from the edge of the Arctic Circle. Also, he'd contemplated becoming a teacher when he'd been younger.

A visual surfaced of Danny, dressed in a striped dress shirt with the sleeves rolled up, teaching about numerators and denominators or the foundations of government to a class of middle schoolers.

Damn, that was hot. It shouldn't have been. But Mike could picture this man doing anything and he'd get warm under the collar.

"I can see you at the front of a classroom," Mike said.

"Yeah?" Danny said, marking an O in one of the corner boxes. "Bit of a long-past dream now. I'm closer to retirement than to starting a new career."

"Lies," Mike said. "Ranchers never retire."

"Well, this one will at some point," Danny mumbled. "It's okay. I'm not sitting here lamenting a lost opportunity. I enjoy my work. But I do wonder sometimes about what my life would look like if I'd made a different choice."

"You would have been great. You're good with kids."

Danny's gaze shuttered. His jaw tightened. "I would have figured it out, but I wouldn't say I'm a natural."

"You sure?" Mike said, shooting a pointed look from Danny to the tic-tac-toe game he'd so kindly started.

Raking a hand through his thick hair, Danny sighed. "Can't say I grew up with many kid-focused male role models."

"So it's hard to see it in yourself?"

"Something along those lines."

Mike wanted to jump to Danny's defense. But what if he was seeing what he wanted to see rather than what was actually there? Was he exaggerating the meaning of Danny's small interactions with Cody and seamless integration into a day on Cooper Ranch, to cling to the possibility of something bigger to look forward to in the future?

He didn't have time to dwell. Barb sashayed up with a tray laden with a rainbow of pie selections and milkshakes topped with so much whipped cream, it was a miracle they weren't drifting toward the ceiling like clouds in a breeze.

After thanking the waitress and splitting the desserts and milkshakes, they dug in.

"There's no way we're going to be hungry for dinner," Mike lamented once his plate only held crumbs and his glass was streaked with the memory of the decadent ice-cream treat.

Danny lounged back in the booth, his long legs tangled with Mike's under the table. "I was a bad influence."

"You sure are," Mike replied. Oops. He had *not* checked the suggestiveness in his tone.

Luckily, his nephew was oblivious.

By the pink in Danny's cheeks, though, *he* was well aware.

"I gotta pee," Cody said, then climbed over Mike and darted to the bathroom.

Danny pressed his knee against Mike's, the contact a slow rise and fall, leaving a comet's tail of sparks all the way along Mike's leg.

"I owe you an apology," Danny said. "I've made a mess of your routine this week."

"No way. I wouldn't have changed a moment we've shared."

His admission earned a relieved smile that quickly turned expectant.

"It's not over yet." Danny straightened and reached across the table, twining his fingers in Mike's. "We have tomorrow night. And whatever we figure out beyond it."

"We could have tonight, too."

"You sure? One of these days, you're going to need to get some actual sleep."

"Sleep's overrated." Especially when he was getting down to hours with Danny in town.

"I could come your way again," Danny murmured.

"Cody and I always talk to Maggie on Thursday nights—she's a couple hours ahead of us. And given he seems a little off kilter this afternoon, I want to make sure we don't cut our conversation short. Would nine be too late?"

"I assume it is for you."

He assumed right. But with each languid stroke of Danny's thumb, Mike cared less and less.

"If you came out and stayed, we'd need to wake up way before Cody. You could be out the door before he noticed." Doubt slipped in. "What am I thinking, though? You've already paid for your night at the hotel."

Danny's thumb paused in the middle of a delicious circle. "My hotel room doesn't come with a beautiful man to sleep with. *Priorities*."

Heat smoldered along the angled planes of his face, arresting Mike's breath in his throat. He couldn't look away. "Danny, I—"

An arm swooped in, cleaning up their dishes with the speed of someone who'd been slinging plates for decades.

"Oh, my word, don't you two look cozy," Barb said, eyes

sparkling. "I'm almost sorry to interrupt. It's been a while since our Michael's held hands with someone in the diner."

Her tone was light but protective, and going off the analytical scrunch to Danny's eyebrows, he caught the waitress's implied message.

"I'll take good care of him, ma'am."

"See that you do." She winked before ferrying the dishes to the kitchen.

Danny watched her retreat, then turned his face to Mike. "I will, you know. Specifically, at 9:01 tonight."

The thumb strokes started up again, and Mike lost half his brain cells.

"I don't think that's what she meant by 'take care,'" he mumbled.

"No kidding," Danny said dryly. "I heard her loud and clear and made no false promises. But lucky for you, I can multi-task."

Chapter Fifteen

Mike eased back on his couch, having sent Cody up to get into his pajamas a minute ago. Their conversations with Maggie were getting longer and longer as the months went on, and the strain caused by the distance showed on his sister's face on the laptop screen.

The minute she'd appeared in the browser, the skin at the nape of Mike's neck had started to prickle, and he couldn't shake it.

"Homesick, Mags?" he said. "Or are you still under the weather?"

He'd waited to ask the question, knowing she tended to downplay anything worrisome around Cody.

She pinched the bridge of her nose and swore under her breath. "I'm just tired, Mike. The work is unending, and the stress builds up. Headaches, fatigue… You know how it is. You can't tell me you're not achy and exhausted after working with Dad during the day and then picking up a shift at night. Or hell, doing the regular after-school-to-dinner-to-bedtime routine. It's tiring enough."

Her lip wobbled.

"Maggie?" he said gently. "Keep talking."

"I miss our routine at home." She dashed the heels of her hands across her cheekbones. "I love being here, helping other moms care for their health and their kids' health. It's *vital*, and the sacrifice on all our parts is worth it, but I want to be with my own kid."

"We knew there would be hard days," he said. There were on his end, too, though he didn't want to burden his sister with his own woes while she was teetering between crying and sobbing.

"Sure, but I didn't know I'd feel like crap like this," she said. "I didn't expect the exhaustion. And it's so damn hot and humid—I keep running a fever. And my digestion… Well, you're the same way when you're stressed. I'll let you connect those dots."

The prickling at his neck spread into a full body shiver. "Maggie, are you sure you shouldn't see a medical professional? Have you talked to the clinic doctor?"

"Already have." She pressed her lips together.

"And?"

"She's running some bloodwork for me, but it takes time."

"Ah." Mike sank back farther into the couch and gripped the throw pillow he'd been using as an elbow rest.

She narrowed her eyes. "You're the one who suggested I see a doctor, and now you're unhappy I did?"

"No, I'm nervous something is wrong, Maggie. I don't like how you have to wait. You're my *twin*. I want you to be okay *now*."

"If only life worked that way."

"Yeah, no kidding," he said.

After blowing her nose with a tissue, she said, "Tell me something happy. Who's this Danny? Cody wouldn't shut up about him."

"He's…" The knot of uncertainty wrapped in hope sitting in his chest was hard to explain. "Well, he's from Bronco—"

She waved her hand for him to move along. "I don't need his name, rank and serial number. Cody gave me a damn dissertation on the guy's basic info. Tell me the good stuff. Does the little twinkle in your eye mean what I think it does?"

He made a face at her. "What *do* you think it means?"

"You're falling for him," she crowed, her usual vivacity brightening her face for a few seconds before dropping away with a queasy looking wince.

"It hasn't been long enough to 'fall' for him." Though from day one, all those months ago, his gut had told him Danny was something special.

"For crying out loud, Mike. You don't get to choose how fast these things happen."

"I'm afraid of being disappointed again," he admitted.

Her expression softened. "Of course. You weren't 'disappointed' before. You were heartbroken."

"Well, it appears I have a type—handsome guys from out of town who could buy and sell our family four times over," he lamented.

"Only four? I thought he was a Taylor."

"Fine, forty."

"More accurate, but still irrelevant. Is he open and attentive with you? Does he have a good heart?" she asked. "I mean, really, he should worship the ground you walk on. Compared to what's out there in the dating wilds, you are a *catch*."

Mike wasn't convinced. What did he have to offer Danny? "If you say so, Mags."

Thumps sounded on the stairs.

"Cody's ready for bed, I take it?" Maggie said.

Mike nodded. "And I'm expecting company in an hour."

She squealed. "Excellent! Don't do anything I wouldn't do."

"You're okay with me having a guest while Cody's in the house?"

"We went over this before I left, Mike," she said. "Nothing's changed. Lock the door and keep the noise down, but live your life. I plan to when I get home."

Hours later, Mike was cocooned in a pair of strong arms, drifting toward sleep. He and Danny had both put their boxers back on after cleaning up a little, but it still left swathes of bare skin to enjoy against his own.

"You're sure it's okay if I stay?" The delicious rumble of words was sleepy, sated, a timbre Mike felt deep along his spine.

The damn bed could have been on fire, and he wouldn't have suggested they get out of it.

Hell, they *had* lit the bed on fire not long ago.

"I have the alarm set for four thirty," he said.

Danny groaned and tightened his embrace. His shoulder served as an excellent pillow, in Mike's opinion.

"For someone who grew up on a ranch, you don't seem like a natural early riser," Mike said.

"I'm not. Why do you think I shifted into management?"

"Oh, I don't know. I figured you were too pretty to hide in a barn. I bet that face makes Taylor Beef *allllll* the money."

Danny snorted. "I'm not in sales, Michael."

Much like Danny had insisted he liked Mike shortening *Daniel* with a nickname, Mike liked hearing *Michael* on the other man's lips.

"You haven't called me by my full name before."

"Barb used it. I liked it. Very archangelic."

"Is that even a word?"

"I think so, but even if it isn't, I'm a staunch believer anything can be turned into an adjective or adverb."

Huh. Not something Mike would have guessed. Learning new things about Danny drew him in even further.

"Got a thing for sword-bearing immortals?" he murmured.

"I have a thing for *you*."

The jitters in Mike's chest settled. He didn't want to stop staring at the perfect angle of the jaw a few inches from his face, but his eyelids felt like they weighed a hundred pounds. He let them drift shut.

I am getting way too serious. Do I really even know him?

And yet…he'd never felt so secure. How could snuggling in these arms be wrong?

* * *

Daniel was on his way out of his hotel room to walk to Castillo's for dinner Friday night, when his phone vibrated.

Seth: I'm going to call, and you're going to answer

Seth: So long as you're done with your midlife crisis

Seth: Hell, even if you're still in the throes of it

Midlife crisis? His brother could screw right off. Hanging his head, he groaned and leaned against the wall by the door.

The phone buzzed again, and he answered it.

"Now?" he snapped.

"Hello to you, too." *Asshole* went unsaid, but it was in Seth's tone.

"Look, I'm on my way out—"

"You can't spare a few minutes? Mom's sure you've been kidnapped. She's been waiting for a ransom note for days."

"You make it sound like I haven't been responding to your texts," Daniel said.

"Anyone can respond to texts. It could have been a ruse."

"Oh, screw off. I've talked to Mom *and* Dad." More like got a guilt trip dropped on him by his dad.

I'm disappointed in your priorities, son.

He'd been too fed up not to snap back. His truth—*I've been disappointed in you for decades, Dad*—had been a long time coming.

Thaddeus had immediately shifted the conversation back to Triple T business, but the fact that he hadn't responded with bluster made Daniel wonder if his words had landed somewhere they might create change.

"Dad's choked that I'm on holidays this week, but I'm done with him thinking he gets a say in my life. I show up and do my job well, and I'm owed this time off. And I—and you, too, by the way—deserve the chance to separate out what truly matters from the *Taylor men work Taylor land* crap we've been fed since we were toddlers."

"I agree. And I'll back you up with Dad however you want me to." Seth sighed. "I wish you'd given me a call, too, though."

"I'm leaving for North Dakota tomorrow. No more delays." He was going to have to drag his heart with him, kicking and screaming, but he couldn't put it off any longer.

"I shifted those meetings to Sunday," Seth said.

"Hang on," Daniel said. "You're getting after me for re-scheduling, but you—"

"Ease up. We're going to look at a piece of property right near where you are."

"What? When?"

"Tomorrow. There's a stretch of land near Tenacity listed for a steal, and I want to set eyes on it," Seth said. "The area doesn't have much going for it at the moment, but it's too damn cheap not to at least consider. With an influx of capital, it might have potential."

"What's it called?" *Please, not anything near Cooper Ranch.*

"Bar J."

The confirmation didn't help him relax much. It wasn't like he was meeting with Mike's dad or even one of the Coopers' neighbors, but it was close enough.

"I don't want to buy in this area, Seth." He didn't want to do anything to risk Mike lumping him in with the ex-boyfriend who had hurt Mike so badly. He needed to aim his investments elsewhere.

Then again, if Daniel bought land in North Dakota, it would make their relationship even more long distance.

"Why the hell not?" Seth said. "It's a better deal than any of the properties in North Dakota, and it's closer to home."

"I—"

How was he supposed to explain his willingness to pass up a good business prospect with his own flesh and blood because of a man he couldn't even call his boyfriend yet?

"If we don't pursue this, I think Taylor Beef will," Seth said.

Goddamn it. What would be worse—Daniel taking this meeting on his own accord, or having it look like he was repping Taylor Beef? Probably the second. "Okay. Fine. We can take a look."

And he would find a reason not to move forward with it.

As for setting off Mike's fears, they'd could talk it through. So long as Daniel explained himself, Mike would understand.

"Look, I have to go. I have...dinner plans."

Seth snorted. "I figured a guy might be part of it. I'd be applauding you for finally finding someone to have dinner with if it wasn't getting in the way of our months of planning."

"My delays aren't about someone else. It's about me—" This was not the kind of thing he got into with his siblings. Life was easier when he kept his private life separate from family. "Hell, you don't need details. I'll see you tomorrow."

He hung up. If Seth was joining him early, he was short on time and long on expectations. His last night in Tenacity needed to leave Mike both satisfied and wanting more. Daniel couldn't imagine leaving for good in the morning.

Chapter Sixteen

No matter Daniel's concerns about bringing a partner into the fold of his own family, he sure was enjoying each moment he got to spend with Mike's. With Mike's friends, technically, though Jenna seemed close enough for Mike to classify her as family. Diego's sister, Nina, seemed like a gem, too. The siblings were full of smiles, trading cheerful jabs in between chatter about their weeks. They'd all had a small world moment when they'd realized that Daniel's sister Eloise's husband was one of Diego and Nina's cousins.

Noise filled the Tenacity Social Club. Every chair was occupied, and tables overflowed with drinks and snacks and laughter.

Perfect for a good time, not so much for finding a quiet moment to take Mike aside and explain Seth's phone call. It wasn't a conversation for the bathroom hallway of a bar, nor could he pull Mike outside for some privacy with the game due to start any minute. But the delay didn't sit right.

"Mike?" he said quietly as they squished around a table, five adults for four spaces. They were holding hands, and he gave Mike's a little squeeze.

A guileless expression met his own nervous one. Mike clearly picked up on it, because his eyebrows knitted and his fingers tensed. "You okay?"

"Oh, yeah. But after trivia—can we talk?"

Mike paled. "Oh. Uh… I guess? I mean, of course. I've been expecting you to…to need to talk."

It sounded like he was walking to the gallows. Damn, why had Daniel picked those specific words? They *always* meant doom.

"Shit, I didn't mean to sound ominous. It's nothing bad. But with me leaving tomorrow, we should talk logistics, you know? For when we can see each other next?"

It was *one* of the things he wanted to discuss, anyway.

"Ahh." The other man's shoulders dropped by a few inches. His grip loosened in Daniel's "Yes. Good idea. Really good. I like *next*."

Daniel exhaled. He'd laid the groundwork, at least.

Everyone around his table was relaxed. His unfinished business made it hard to mimic their casual energy.

Diego was sprawled in his chair and had an arm stretched along the back of Jenna's. He was stroking lazy circles on her shoulder and looked as satisfied as a well-fed lion in a patch of sun.

Daniel recognized the feeling. His own smile kept drifting into *smug bastard* territory. Guaranteed, no one in the bar had a man as amazing as Mike Cooper at their side.

Their clasped hands hung between their chairs. Not hidden, but not advertising things for the entire bar's entertainment.

He was erring on being protective of Mike. Knowing how much the folks in Tenacity seemed to like to keep track of each other's business, he figured obvious PDA would invite curious interruptions all night long.

Better to focus on impressing Mike's group of friends rather than the whole town. The easiest way to ease his way into the trio seemed to be to cover a round or two and to be as much of a secret weapon with trivia as possible. His ability to impress would depend on the questions.

"Do we know the categories ahead of time?" he asked.

Mike nodded.

Jenna, red hair pinned up and wearing a simple dress in a nod to what she'd announced was a rare kid-free Friday night out, was busy making sure her pen worked and confirming the answer sheets were in order.

"Five rounds." She flicked through the photocopied pages, narrating as she went. "Famous Georges, musical decades, four-letter words—oh, you'll be good at that one, Mike—"

"No better than you," he interrupted, scowling playfully at his best friend.

She flipped the last two papers and made a face. "Mythical creatures and…fish?"

"The quilting circle was in charge of the categories," Mike explained.

"One of the quilters is a big angler?" Daniel asked.

"Might have been Cecil Brewster, but could have been Ellen," Jenna said.

"As in your mom?" Daniel smiled at the thought of her executing a perfect fly cast into a river.

"Taught me everything I know." Mike beamed. "Ties the best flies in the county, as far as I'm concerned. The creek on our property's a bit small for any serious fishing, though. Each year when I was growing up, she'd take Maggie and me on a trip west to the Gallatin River. We'd stock up our freezer for months."

"All right," Nina said, a competitive sparkle in her eyes. "You've got fish under control, and four-letter words could be anything. Daniel, are you going to be our ringer in any of the other categories? Big music buff, maybe? An expert in Georges?"

"I can handle any nineties bands," he said. "And I've read my fair share of fantasy novels."

Nina perked up. "Hobbits, dragon riders or immortal faeries?"

He couldn't help but feel it was a test.

"Uh, all of the above," he said.

Jenna tuned in, too. "On a scale of people riding dragons to people *riding* dragons, where do you land?"

"Jenna," Mike warned, squeezing Daniel's hand.

He squeezed back. The question was silly, but he figured their willingness to get a little off-color with him was a good sign.

"You mean shifters, or just people and dragons?" Daniel asked.

"Shifters would be in the middle," Jenna said.

"Then I'd be on the 'dragons as transportation' end of the spectrum, but I try to keep an open mind when it comes to books." He eyed her with suspicion. Nina, too, who was listening raptly. "Did I pass this particular exam?"

Diego snorted into his beer.

Mike's face was flushed. "You don't need to humor them."

Daniel leaned in and whispered, "I like it. They're figuring out if I'm good enough for you. You deserve that."

"You don't have to earn your place," Mike insisted.

"Yes, he does!" Jenna exclaimed, but the genuine smile on her face and the gentle pat she gave Daniel's forearm assured him she was joking.

"Jenna."

She waved off Mike's complaint. "One more. Last one, I promise."

Lifting his free hand palm up, Daniel curled his fingers in a *bring it on* gesture.

"*Die Hard* or *The Sound of Music*?" Jenna said.

"Those two aren't connected, cariño," Diego said, chuckling.

Inspiration struck, and Daniel laughed. "No, they are," he said. "The correct answer is *a double header in December* because they're both Christmas movies. I mean, I know *The Sound of Music* isn't about Christmas at all, but it was always on TV then, so I'll always consider it one."

Jenna slow clapped. "Ooh, he's *smart*, Mike."

Mike's half smile was tender. "Why do you think I brought him to trivia?"

They chatted for a few more minutes until a man around Daniel's age took the microphone, welcomed the teams and made sure all their names were written up on the portable whiteboard near the bar. He ran them through the rules, and then they were off.

They got the first four famous Georges, coming up with George Harrison, George Clooney, George Foreman and Regina George. The fifth question was trickier.

"The George who held the record for most home runs in a decade?" Jenna repeated, looking baffled.

Daniel dug into his baseball trivia and unearthed the right answer.

"Babe Ruth."

She scribbled down the response and let out a whoop when it was confirmed correct.

Mike leaned in close, pressing their shoulders together. Daniel was hoping for a kiss but was going to let Mike be the initiator there, and he stopped out of lip reach. "I'm impressed. Though I guess it's to be expected given you're a baseball star."

"I *was* a baseball *player*," he corrected. "And I was on a winning team. I wasn't a star."

"A more important trophy is the one sitting on the bar," Jenna said, pointing to the gold statue.

"Is that a spray-painted garden statue?" Daniel squinted in the low lighting. "A...hedgehog?"

"A *prize* garden-statue hedgehog," Nina corrected.

Questionable trophy aside, Daniel appreciated their competitiveness.

They held their own for round two, with four out of five on musical decades. Four-letter words were their undoing, though.

"Did the quilting club comb the dictionary for obscure

words?" Jenna complained. "We're in *second*. I can't believe we got four wrong."

"Danny got *adze* for us at least," Mike said.

"You need to come through on fish, Mike," Nina said.

The emcee was in the middle of giving the five-minute warning about said category when a hand clapped on Daniel's shoulder.

"Ha! Found you," a familiar voice said.

A familiar voice *not* supposed to be here yet.

Daniel turned, then drew back. Not only Seth loomed over his chair. Their younger brother, Ryan, stood close behind.

"Didn't take us long to hunt you down," Ryan said, a big smile on his face. "We assumed you'd be at the hotel, but the person at the front desk thought you might be here, given it's the hottest ticket in town tonight."

All fine, but *they* weren't supposed to be in Tenacity. Not tonight.

Damn it. His pulse picked up, and he pinned his brothers with a pointed look, trying to will them not to mention the meeting he and Seth were taking in Tenacity. He had to be the one to frame it for Mike.

Mike was holding his beer bottle with both hands, confusion on his handsome face. He smiled at the new arrivals. "Danny's brothers, I assume?"

"You got it. And you must be 'dinner plans,'" Seth said in true younger-brother form. He and Daniel were only two years apart, but Seth still loved to grind his gears.

"You look younger than me," Ryan said offhandedly.

Mike's face turned uncertain. His friends winced.

"Damn, Ry. Thanks for that." Daniel put an arm around Mike. Ryan wasn't wrong—at thirty-four, he *was* older than Mike—but the truth didn't make his comment necessary. "Clearly, the extra years you've spent on the earth weren't devoted to manners."

"Sorry." Ryan's cheeks were red. "When did we last see you with someone new, though? Especially someone who's nowhere near—"

"How about instead of a beer, we get you a shovel?" Daniel said. "So you can dig yourself as deep as you want."

Seth was suppressing a laugh.

"Don't pretend you're innocent in all this." Daniel sent Seth a pointed look.

His brother held up his hands in surrender. "I just want a key to your hotel room."

Daniel ignored the request. He had some introductions to take care of before Mike's friends started to think him rude.

"This is Mike," Daniel said, waiting while his brothers shook hands with Mike, who settled back into the crook of his arm. Daniel then went around the table, introducing the rest of the group. "And these are my brothers, Seth and Ryan. Seth and I are driving to North Dakota tomorrow, and for whatever reason, he's early. And Ryan is…"

"Seth's taxi service," Ryan filled in. "No point in having two vehicles here."

"You two should join us. More help with fish and mythical creatures," Jenna said cheerfully. "Pull up a chair!"

"Thanks, but I don't want to horn in," Seth said.

"You weren't answering your texts," Ryan said to Daniel.

"We're in the middle of a cutthroat trivia competition." Daniel waved a hand at the whiteboard. "It's against the rules to be on my phone."

"We don't want to kill your vibe," Ryan said.

"Mmm, yeah, that's clear," Daniel said.

Diego laughed. "Brothers, right?"

Nina elbowed him. "Sisters, too. I *love* killing Diego's vibe."

"You're sure you don't want to stay for a drink? Round four's about to start," Mike said.

"Thanks, but Ryan needs to get back to his wife, and my stuff's in his truck. So long as Daniel calls the hotel and has my name put on the reservation, I can tuck in for the night."

Daniel's ears started to buzz. "Uh, hold up. I didn't know that in asking for a key to my room, you planned to share it with me."

"Why pay for two?" Seth said.

"Because I'm *using* that one?"

"It's okay." Mike leaned into Daniel's ear. "You can come home with me instead."

"Right." He took a deep breath. Mike's place would work. And the quicker his brothers left, the better. Pulling out his wallet, he fumbled for the key card and handed it to Seth. "Here. Fill your boots. I'll see you in the morning."

"Make sure to come get me in time," Seth said. "We need to be at the Bar J by eight thirty."

Daniel cursed under his breath. "Yeah, well, we'll see."

"Oh, here's question number one," Jenna cut in. "Medusa was a… Quick, folks."

Mike was ignoring her. His wary gaze was fixed on Daniel. "The Bar J?"

"The Bar J is not a mythical creature, Mike," Jenna said, pen poised over the paper.

The teasing comment earned her a mighty glare.

"Medusa was a gorgon," Daniel answered Jenna's prompt by rote, keeping his gaze on Mike. "It's a long story, but—"

"But nothing. What meeting do you have at the Bar J?"

Daniel cupped Mike's shoulder. "I didn't want to have any meeting there—"

"Hang on." Ryan scowled hard enough to scare a class of kindergartners. At least it was focused on Seth, not Daniel. "I left my wife on a Friday night to drive your ass here, and he's not even interested?"

"No," Seth corrected, "you drove me here because he and I are meeting Realtors all weekend. And given how much work's been done on his truck this week—" he shot Daniel a suspicious look "—it's in pristine condition for a drive across state lines, so I didn't need to bring mine."

By the disbelief spreading on Mike's face, Daniel wasn't going to need his truck to make the trip east. Mike was going to give him the boot so hard, he'd land in Lake Michigan.

"Mike, it's not what you think," he said.

"Oh, because that phrase isn't a red flag for lies and excuses." Mike's expression hardened. "Speaking of excuses— excuse me."

He shoved his chair back, jarring Daniel's arm, and stormed toward the exit.

Everyone at the table, including Ryan and Seth, now standing awkwardly, gaped after Mike.

"I'd better go talk to him," Daniel said. "And question two is *wyvern*."

"Huh?" Jenna said.

"Two-legged, dragon-like creature—wyvern."

"As if that matters!" she said.

"I've already ruined Mike's night," he said, standing. "I don't want to wreck your game, too."

He chased after Mike, knowing he'd destroyed more than just the evening.

The second Mike got to the top of the stairs, he strode in the direction of his truck. He'd had to park a couple blocks down the street, given the crowd attending trivia. With any luck, the distance wouldn't give anyone the chance to catch up to him. He didn't want comfort from any of his friends. In particular, he didn't want more excuses from Danny.

The slight chill to the evening air should have been a relief for his hot, prickly skin, but nothing could break through the emotions churning through him. His internal warning signal was screaming louder than his cell phone during a county emergency alert.

Why the hell was his heart threatening to crack in half?

Because I trusted someone I shouldn't have. Again.

When the hell was he going to start listening to his instincts to protect himself instead of falling for a man who had seemed sweet and dependable and honest? What a freaking facade.

"Mike, wait!" Jogging footsteps echoed on the pavement behind him. Dress boots, even more high-end than the pristine ones Danny had worn out to the ranch all week.

Those boots belonged to *Daniel*, not Danny.

A goddamn illusion, when Danny was yet another guy hiding his true motivations.

Muttering a few words from his not-in-front-of-Cody lexicon, he ignored Danny's second "Wait!" and yanked his keys out of his pocket.

"Mike, I wasn't trying to keep it from you. It just wasn't the kind of conversation I wanted to have in front of your friends," Danny said, finally catching up to Mike. "They were already with you when I got to the restaurant, and then we were at the Social Club, which was packed. It's why I mentioned needing to talk later."

He wasn't breathing hard, but a flush stained his face. That goddamn devastating face. Mike was going to be seeing it in his dreams for *years*.

"No, you said you wanted to talk about when we were going to see each other next." Mike nearly spat the words.

"It's all connected. My brothers' arrival was a surprise to me, too." Danny laced his fingers together and braced them at the back of his head, sending his thick waves askew.

Mike didn't want to notice those details. Didn't want to *want* those details.

Not from someone who knew the precise location of Mike's sore points and still stabbed a poker into the lingering wounds.

"You knew about the meeting, so *that* wasn't a surprise," he managed.

Danny groaned. "Seth sprang it on me a few minutes before I left for dinner. I thought we were headed straight for North Dakota, but he crammed in a tour of the Bar J. I told him I wasn't interested."

"And yet you're going."

"Yes, to convince him it's not right for him and me or for Taylor Beef. Or for Tenacity. No matter if the property is promising, it's not worth you thinking I've been spending my time in Tenacity ingratiating myself in your life and in town for the sake of a business deal."

"*Is* that what you've been doing? Ingratiating yourself? All your *aw, shucks* smiles at the diner and helping my dad and playing along with Jenna's and Nina's questions about books?"

"No! I mean, of course I wanted to make a good impression… But because I want to be important to *you*."

Okay. That was rational. And sweet. But was it real?

Mike took a deep breath.

If Danny was telling the truth, then why was Mike finding it impossible to calm down? He felt like a soda can that had been dropped on the floor. If he opened up, he'd fizz all over, a sticky, foaming mess no one wanted to clean up.

"What else are you hiding?"

"Mike…" Danny extended a hand toward him, then withdrew it with a sigh. "Things went sideways tonight, and I want to fix them."

He studied the other man. Two sets of footsteps rang out from the other side of the road, headed in the direction of the hotel. Mike glanced over. Danny's brothers, pointedly looking away from Mike and Danny, were giving them a wide berth for their conversation. Kind of them, considering how they'd been the ones to shine light on this whole problem.

"It's the second time this week you've kept something from me."

"It's…do you really think it's the same thing? Does waiting a few hours for a private conversation really count as *hiding*?"

Something crumpled in his chest. Danny was right. It wasn't the same. So why was he reacting as if it was?

"I don't know. But it feels like—" he mumbled a curse "—I was waiting for the moment, the sign marking 'the end.' And this felt like it."

Shadows cast the angles of Danny's face into a mask of disbelief. "Okay. That's how you protect yourself, and believe me, I understand how being hurt in the past has made you gun-shy. But I was hoping…hoping you'd see that *I'm* not here to hurt you."

Mike inhaled, trying to reason his way past his initial panic. Danny *had* been clear about needing to talk. Hell, when he'd mentioned it, Mike had gotten scared, thinking *that* meant the end. Why couldn't he fully trust the man he'd gotten to know? The man he could see caring deeply about?

"You wanted something *temporary,*" Mike reminded him. "Which makes sense. We come from opposite worlds. I'll never have the ability to up and make appointments for major real-estate deals—"

"I only need you to be you." Danny's voice shook, tearing at Mike's heart with every quaver. "Please, believe me. I wasn't going to let us fall asleep tonight without telling you about the Bar J. Including how I'm *not* intending to buy it. I know how protective you are over Tenacity, and I never want you to think I'm trying to swoop in and take advantage of our relationship."

"I do believe you. But it doesn't change how we don't move in the same spaces. Cattle conventions and business schmoozing—how could I be a meaningful part of that? Not with what you said about your dad not accepting you. He'll *never* accept me."

"Which is why I want to keep you separate from all that, Mike. What if I want to fit into *your* life?"

"Why would you?"

"Because I want to love you, damn it!"

Time just…stopped. The beams from the street lights hung in the air like illuminated dust motes. All sound cut out, and Mike's heart stopped for a second, so desperate to be loved by Daniel Taylor.

No. No way was it a real possibility.

"You can't say you love me," he croaked. "Not this soon."

"I'm not. I said I *want* to love you. Quality doesn't come from a rush job, Mike, and with you, I want to create something precious. Unbreakable."

"But…" The lump at the back of Mike's throat was making it hard to get the words out. "You have big responsibilities waiting for you back in Bronco. Your brothers depend on you. And it's obvious you love them." He blinked hard to keep the tears back.

"Sure. Nothing insurmountable, though."

"Isn't it? To keep everything separate… How? When you take what's left of you after you've met all your responsibilities and what's left of me after I've dealt with mine, there's not much 'quality' left over."

"Ah."

"I don't think there's enough to build a real relationship on," Mike said, choking on the truth. "Love is too important to do it wrong. And if I'm not careful… I can't be someone's boy toy again."

Danny stumbled back a step. "What? You think I see you so frivolously?"

"You wouldn't be the first."

"I'm starting to have real feelings for you. I thought you felt the same way."

"I did—the guy I've hung out with all week is too easy to fall for. But is the person you've tried to be while here really *you*? You keep compartmentalizing parts of your life, controlling the way you dole out dribs and drabs of your existence.

And I get why. Your father's a piece of work, and you have a lot to manage, there. But I need to know all of you. And if you're playing a role—'Danny who fits into Tenacity'—then we're not building something real."

"What is it, Mike? We won't have time for each other? Or you think I'm being dishonest about who I am?"

Mike leaned back against the passenger door and let his head fall against the sheet metal with a *thunk*. With Maggie struggling, his family needed him to be strong right now. Even if he had to pretend. "It's all of it. It's too much."

Danny's laugh was crackling dry. "And here I thought I wasn't going to be enough for you."

"Same." Mike swallowed, trying to keep his voice level. "Am I wrong, though?"

Danny stood, hands limp at his sides. And the longer his mouth gaped, the more Mike knew he wasn't going to like the answer.

Chapter Seventeen

Daniel paced in a circle on the sidewalk. With Mike leaning against his truck, it was hard to know where to stand.

If Mike's accusations hadn't been enough to sweep Daniel's feet out from under him, realizing he'd gotten to the age of forty-four and was about to have to reexamine his entire existence would have done it.

You keep compartmentalizing...

Mike was not wrong.

The whole time Daniel had been here in Tenacity, he'd been ignoring his life in Bronco. And it wasn't about needing a break from real life.

He'd been concealing—or at least downplaying—parts of his life, and it was time to break the damn pattern.

"What do you want to know?" Daniel said, not caring if his voice was breaking. "The barriers you're seeing... What parts of me do you want to see?"

"It's not about hiding." Mike slashed a hand through the air. "It's about you being a different person when you're here. You're not going to be able to keep that up forever. My life isn't role play."

"What if the person I've been while I'm here makes me happier than I've ever been?"

"Who's going to live the whole other life you have in Bronco, then? Who's going to be the oldest son and the HR expert and the mentor?"

The mention of each role was a punch, each from a different direction, sending his mind in a spin. "I… I know I need to get back to work. But I also need *you*. I'm a resourceful man, Mike. I told you, if there's a way to be with you, either in Bronco or Tenacity or some combination of both, I will make it happen."

"You must have missed the faulty equation, then. Because you wanting to make it happen, or even wanting to fall in love with me, doesn't find a place for Cody and me in your life."

"It will if I make one," Daniel said.

"Oh, yeah? He and I are going to be able to show up for family holidays? Sit around your dining table like we're actual members of the Taylor brood?"

Protectiveness rose in his chest, as vicious as one of the mythical creatures he'd identified for the trivia round. "Well, no."

"That's what I thought," he whispered.

Daniel rocked on his heels. "Why would you want to?"

"Because that's what people do when they fall in love! They share their lives."

"Not if it means putting the person I love in a position where they could get hurt! Who the hell knows what my dad would say, and I care too much about both of you to put you in harm's way." He let out a slow breath, trying to calm down, to remain rational. In no world could he handle the thought of opening Mike or Cody up to the rejection and lack of acceptance Daniel himself had faced from Thaddeus Taylor. The rest of his family wasn't like that, though. He could at least bring Mike into that part of the fold. "My siblings and my mom would welcome you with open arms. We can do things with them without my dad around. And *your* family already accepts us, no questions asked."

Mike's smile was soft, anguished. "You've seen my parents this week. There are no divisions with them. And if we fall in love, your struggles will be my struggles, too. But that will be impossible if you don't share it with me. Can you be all in, if you don't let me live all the parts of your life with you?"

All in.

When it came down to it, Daniel hadn't done that before.

"The last thing I want to do is try to let you in, and then fail and be one more jerk who hurt you," he said.

"So then, why are we going in circles over this?"

For the first time since they'd started arguing tonight, Daniel didn't have a good answer. Holding Mike's gaze, so full of indecisive yearning, was like trying to keep a hot coal in his grip.

Lifting a hand, he reached for the one man for whom he'd *wanted* to break down his walls.

Mike didn't turn away, accepting Daniel's cupped palm on his cheek with a hiss of breath.

"I am so scared of failing you," Daniel said, savoring the warmth of Mike's skin against his. "*But*, what if I don't? Let's say I figure out how to be 'all in.' Would you be able to trust it?"

Beautiful brown eyes blinked open, a glimmer of a future in their depths. "Would you…would you give me some time to figure that out?"

"Yes. Giving you time is easy. Hell, you make me want to find a way to give you the damn world."

"I don't want *the* world, Daniel. I just want to be a part of yours."

"Being a part of it isn't enough. You deserve to be at the very center of it," Daniel said.

"Can we make that work?"

We. It was a good place to start. "Not if I keep hiding in Tenacity when my problems are in Bronco. And not without you taking the time you asked for. But I don't want to walk away tonight as if this is the end."

"I…" Turning an inch, Mike brushed his lips against the mound of Daniel's thumb.

Warmth rushed along his skin.

Hopping back into Mike's bed for another night wasn't giving Mike the time he'd asked for. Daniel intended to head for his hotel room alone.

But if he left without one last kiss, he'd regret it forever.

He lowered his head, meeting Mike's waiting, parted lips with a tender brush.

The shock of pleasure was minuscule in comparison to the yearning in Daniel's chest. It would have to be enough until Mike took the time he needed and found his answers.

Were they just delaying an inevitable end?

Daniel had to cling to the hope they'd find a way, otherwise he'd never find the strength to leave.

"You know, it wouldn't hurt you to smile at some point, considering you ended up being right," Seth griped.

Daniel glared at his brother, who was taking his turn behind the wheel for the tail end of their four-hour drive to North Dakota.

"I hope you never tell the women in your life to smile more," Daniel said, "because it's *infuriating*."

"So is being stuck in a truck with your sulking, grumpy ass."

"You're no less grumpy after seeing the water-source issues at the Bar J," Daniel pointed out.

Seth frowned. "No wonder they're looking to sell—they're never going to be able to turn a profit on that piece of land."

One more loss for Tenacity. Daniel winced. "Look, I'm glad we're not going to end up on the wrong end of a bad business deal. And yeah, I'm glad you're no longer interested. I'm just not feeling full of sunshine and lollipops today."

"I figured you'd be cranky after we ended up sharing a bed last night." Seth drummed his fingers against the steering wheel. "Want to talk about it?"

"No."

If a solution hadn't materialized while talking it over with Mike, the person who mattered the most, it wasn't going to magically surface by hashing it out with his brother. Well-meaning nature aside, Seth had his own history of being burned by love.

"He was cute," Seth said.

Daniel scowled. Talk about a diminutive description. "Look, I know he's young, but with all the responsibility he's taking on, he's more mature than a lot of men our age. He's funny, smart... So damn kind..."

"Easy, killer. It wasn't a dig. I only meant I can tell he's attractive. But obviously you're drawn to him for more than his looks."

"Oh, it's part of it." Daniel cracked with a sad laugh. "But yeah, his heart matters more."

"And did you manage to win it?"

"I think I could have, were I not living with my head up my ass about what it takes to get close to someone."

Seth huffed out of his nose. "You're talking to the wrong brother. It's Ryan who's full of hot tips about falling in love, or any of our sisters. Can't say I want to be the lone single-ton around the ranch, but then, I don't want to curse you to a life of being alone, either. Not if you want to find someone."

"I think I did find someone." Daniel dropped his head back on the rest.

"He looked at you like he wanted to be found, too. At least until I mentioned the Bar J," Seth said. "I hoped you would have cleared that up with him, the way you tore off out of the bar. Do you need me to vouch for you? Explain you had nothing to do with taking our meeting?"

"No. He believed me on that at least."

"And what did he not believe?"

"My ability to fully include him in my life. Which I don't know how to do without eventually hurting him and his nephew."

Seth's low whistle did nothing to fill the gaping hole in Daniel's gut.

"He's right to be cautious," Daniel defended. "I've never truly opened up every part of myself to a man."

"Yeah, and isn't it a good thing to be able to recognize something like that? Is it fair not to give you the chance to change?"

He stared out the window at the flat plains stretching until they knitted with the infinite blue sky. Endless possibilities, and before Mike, he'd believed he'd shake up his life and discover the meaning he needed through buying his own patch of land with Seth.

Now he couldn't imagine a new adventure without having a particular pair of hazel eyes along for the ride.

"I can understand why he needs to be wary. He has more than his own needs to worry about."

"The nephew," Seth said.

"He's a good kid."

"And you're a good man."

"We weren't raised by one," he mumbled. "At least, not with a good example of how a man should love unconditionally. He'll never—" he swallowed, trying to loosen the tension in his throat "—no matter how many ultimatums Mom gives him, I can't trust Dad not to be surprised if I brought a man home. And if Cody ever saw that…"

"Dad is absolutely in the wrong, Daniel, and we'll keep telling him that until he starts to believe it. But Mike wouldn't be dating our dad. He'd be dating someone who *knows* how to love. And the rest of us would love whoever loves you." The tendons in Seth's knuckles strained on the steering wheel. "It's not fair for you to lose out on something good because of Dad."

Daniel sighed. "No, it's not. But there's more to it than just Taylor ignorance."

"Since when do interpersonal problems trip you up? You solve them all day long at work."

"This isn't the same. It's about figuring out how to meld who I am and what Mike stands for, made worse by the literal miles of difference between us."

"Yikes." Seth exhaled through his teeth. "And here I thought it was a garden-variety midlife crisis."

"Oh, screw off." He slumped farther in his seat and knocked his brother's biceps with his fist.

But Seth's words—*you're a good man*—stuck with him for the rest of the weekend as they toured fields and barns, pastures and paddocks.

All Saturday afternoon and Sunday, Daniel kept waiting for a piece of property to light him on fire—or at minimum to bring the sense of peace he'd gotten riding around Cooper Ranch.

Nothing felt like *his*. Not even on a part-time basis.

And when he closed his eyes on both of the nights they spent at a bed-and-breakfast, he didn't dream of any of the spreads they'd explored. He dreamed about riding a beautiful Appaloosa across a field in Tenacity, side by side with a sexy cowboy mounted on a frisky buckskin.

Monday morning he stood on yet another stretch of asphalt. A silo climbed toward the sky on his right, casting a shadow across a shorter, squatter barn.

"That'll withstand the elements for years," Seth said, shifting in place at Daniel's side. He squinted under the brim of his cream-colored felt hat.

"Maybe so, but we're in the market for more than a barn, and I'm not seeing enough here to take a closer look," Daniel said, pitching his voice for his brother alone.

"One spread was too big, one was too small. This one should

be just right, but somehow it's not. You done playing Goldilocks?" Seth said through gritted teeth.

He flipped Seth the bird.

"Let's head home tonight," Seth grumbled. "No point in sticking around. If you didn't like what we've looked at so far, nothing else is going to be the winner."

"You don't think so?" Daniel asked, wiping sweat from his brow under the midday sun. He'd dressed in long sleeves and a blazer and was regretting the second layer.

"Oh, I think there's a ton of potential in what we've seen. But it's clear you're no longer eager to take on opportunities out of Montana. An idea *you* floated to *me*, I might remind you."

Daniel scowled. "Business is as much about the times you say no as the times you say yes."

The Realtor strode over from where she'd been taking a call. Disappointment simmered under her neutral expression. "This one checked all your boxes on paper. But I'm getting 'not in reality' vibes."

Her *again* went unspoken.

"Doesn't seem so," Seth said. He was almost cheerful in his resignation.

"Dang. I had high hopes you'd fall in love with this one," she said.

"Mmm, my brother already fell in love this week. I suspect he might be full up."

Daniel refused to feel guilty. "I appreciate your time, but I'm not willing to take on this big of an investment without being a hundred percent sold."

"Always smart," the Realtor said.

Ha. Right. The last thing Daniel felt at the moment was "smart."

Once they hit the road, Daniel in the driver's seat this time, Seth didn't say much for the first part of the journey.

Neither did Daniel. He didn't want to poke the bear, given Seth had a valid reason to be pissed about Daniel's about face on the real-estate deals. He squinted into the afternoon light and resigned himself to a quiet drive home.

The silence only gave his brain time to spiral, though. It was going to be damn impossible to drive past Tenacity without stopping.

As they neared the border between states, a cartoon-dinosaur sign loomed on the side of the road, proclaiming it was a mile to the local natural history museum. Daniel chuckled at the silly design. Cody would for sure critique its lack of realism. Not to mention he'd adore the museum. They might have a gift shop the boy would be happy to get lost in, too.

A minute later, he was pulling off at the exit.

"Time to take a leak?" Seth asked.

"Uh, yeah," Daniel said. "I'm going to pop in at that museum. I doubt they'd mind."

And if he happened to drop some cash on a dinosaur model, he knew an eight-year-old who'd love getting a present in the mail.

Chapter Eighteen

"Do you want the good news or the bad?" Maggie asked.

The internet connection was rough this morning, and the video kept buffering. The pauses served to emphasize how ragged Mike's twin looked. She must have lost ten pounds in the past few weeks. The circles under her eyes were so dark they could have been bruises.

His heart was in his damn throat.

More accurately, part of his heart was on the other end of a spotty Wi-Fi call, in need of care and out of his reach.

Mike's mom, who was sitting next to him at his kitchen table, peered out the window, no doubt checking for Cody, who was outside with Mike's father.

"Start at the beginning." Ellen's quiet encouragement carried an air of her experience as a medical professional.

"You know the beginning," Maggie said. "And my symptoms haven't changed. I spent a few days in the hospital this week."

Mike's mom grabbed his hand and clutched it.

"What?" Mike whispered.

"Honey, no," Ellen said. She was cutting off the circulation to Mike's fingers, but he wasn't going to point that out. "Did you get any answers?"

Maggie nodded. "It's a parasite, common to the region."

"Treatable?" Mike asked.

"Yes, but tricky to do so here without being a burden. The antiparasitic treatment is straightforward, but I need testing to make sure it hasn't progressed. If it progresses past the acute phase, it can cause serious problems. I'll need to see a cardiologist and a gastroenterologist… Long story not so short, I'm being sent home."

"For good?" Mike said, glancing in Cody's direction again.

He was still happily tossing a baseball with his grandfather.

Maggie closed her eyes for a second. A visible wave of fatigue washed over her face. When she opened her eyes again, they were damp. "Yes. They have to replace me, and it's uncertain how long it will take for me to recover, so they can't hold the position for me."

Ellen held her free hand to her mouth. "I hate that you're sick. I don't hate that you'll be home safe."

"Same, Mom. Honestly, same." Maggie sighed.

"So, what's next?" Ellen asked, matter-of-fact as always.

It took them a while to run through details and plans. Packing up Maggie's temporary life and getting back to Montana was going to be a strain, but not a long one. She anticipated being home before the end of next week. She wasn't a contagion risk, so she'd be able to fly commercial.

"We'll pick you up at the airport. We'll be the ones with the welcome-home sign," Mike said.

"You're not doing this alone," Ellen said, straightening. "Packing? Navigating layovers? I'm booking a flight down to help you."

"Mom, no," Maggie protested. "I have coworkers who can help me pack. You can't take off work, and Mike needs you there for Cody."

"Maybe I can get Jenna to pitch in," he said.

"For your evening shifts?" his sister asked.

"We'll figure something out. Mom's right. You don't want to be traveling home alone."

"It's a huge expense," Maggie said. She knew as much as anyone the tight financial line her parents walked with the ranch.

"And a worthy one," Ellen insisted. "You might *be* a mom, but you still need your own."

Maggie grimaced. "Speaking of being a mom, I should tell my kid now. I don't like having to explain it over a buffering screen, but it would be too shocking for me to show up with no warning. Especially if you're going to come meet me, Mom. He'd have too many questions about where you were going. And I don't want you all to have to explain it to him on my behalf."

Ellen fetched the boy from the yard, along with Larry.

The three adults sat with Cody as Maggie slowly and patiently explained her illness to her son. He had a bunch of questions about how parasites worked, and Mike had visions of his future involving countless sketches of microscopic organisms littering the kitchen table.

Cody remained matter of fact until Maggie shared her plan to come home.

His eyes filled with tears. "For real?"

"Yeah, baby. For real." She started to sniffle.

"Awesome!" Cody gushed, wiping at the tears of happiness with the side of his hand. "Will you be home Sunday morning? We always have pancakes Sunday morning. Maybe we can have extra syrup?"

Maggie laughed into a Kleenex. "You can have as much syrup as you want."

Mike appreciated how his nephew's mind had gone to one of the traditions they'd kept going in Maggie's absence. Sunday-morning pancakes were one of Mike's favorite parts of the week with Cody. His nephew was getting pretty good at flipping smaller ones.

If Danny was here, how would he fit into Sunday brunch?

Life with Danny gone felt wrong, but so did the idea of not being able to cook for his nephew.

"I can't give either up," he muttered.

His whole family stared at him, including Maggie through the screen.

Ugh, why had he let his thoughts slip out? It was a truth no one else needed to know, especially not now, with Maggie on the call.

"Give what up?" she asked.

"Nothing important."

His mom made a sound like she was seconds away from calling him on his crap, but miracle of miracles, she refrained.

Instead they talked to Maggie for a few more minutes, arranged a time to connect again to go over travel details and cut the connection.

"We'd better let your uncle get to work, lovey," Ellen said to Cody. "Are you ready for Friday-night popcorn and a movie? Oh, and guess what—I picked up our mail, and there's a package with *your* name on it." Her gaze shifted to Mike. "With a Bronco address. Do you want to be there when Cody unwraps it?"

Bronco? Huh? What message was Danny sending by mailing something to Cody alone?

"Can I open it tonight? Please?" Cody begged.

"I'm thinking if Danny *didn't* want you to open it right away, he would have texted me with some instructions," Mike reasoned.

Danny had followed through on his promise to text, and Mike had replied, going back and forth on the mundane and not-so-mundane parts of their lives. Danny's news about deciding North Dakota wasn't the place for him had been a big decision, so it must have ranked higher than alerting Mike to whatever was in Cody's package. Or maybe he'd wanted the present to be a surprise for Mike, too.

A better surprise would be Danny figuring out a way to be in my bed this weekend.

But they had so much more to figure out beyond a quick weekend sleepover.

He'd asked for time for a reason.

"Go for it, Cody," he said thickly. "That'll be something fun for you to do tonight."

"Right," Mike's mom said. "Because it's *nothing important*."

"Right."

"Michael." She cupped his cheek with a warm palm. It carried the scent of the same apricot moisturizer she'd been using since he was a kid. "You can lie to yourself until you're nothing but stardust and dirt, but you cannot lie to your mother and expect her not to notice."

"I'd better get to work, Mom."

"We're putting this conversation on hold, not forgetting about it."

He expected nothing less.

The last thing he wanted to do was sling drinks. His mind swirled from Maggie's health to her return to Cody to Danny...

Danny. Oh, man.

All he wanted was to hear Danny's voice.

Cody plopped down onto the floor by the back door and grabbed his dusty sneakers. Pausing with one of the shoes half-on, he peered up at Mike. "You look sad. Is it because of Mom?"

Fear teased the edges of the boy's expression.

"No, bud," Mike said. "Your mom is safe and in good hands. She'll be home and healthy soon."

"Oh, wait," Cody said. "It's because Danny sent me a present and not you."

He chuckled. "Not that, either. I don't need presents from Danny."

"*Need* is such a strong word," Ellen muttered.

Mike glared at his mom.

"It's okay if you're sad he's not here, Uncle Mike," Cody said, yanking on his shoes.

"Who says I'm sad?" Mike asked, holding out one of Cody's sweatshirts hanging on the hook on the wall next to the door.

"You've been frowning *all* week," Cody replied.

Ellen snorted, sounding beyond vindicated.

Between Cody's uncanny instincts and his mother's all-too-honed ones, he knew when he was cornered.

"Yeah, Cody. I did feel sad this week. It's no fun when someone you care about leaves."

"He had to go home, though, right?" Cody stood and took the sweatshirt.

"He did."

"Why?"

"It's complicated," Mike said. "Adult stuff."

Cody pulled the sweatshirt over his head, sending his curls in ten different directions. Ellen smoothed out the discombobulated strands. Cody ducked away from the fussing.

"*Adult stuff.* Mom always tells me that, too." The boy's face fell. "And she always tells me she misses me, too. But she didn't tonight. Do you think she still does?"

He stepped into his grandma's outstretched arms, accepting a tight squeeze and a hand to the back of his head.

Ellen's usual no-nonsense, nurse's demeanor looked on the verge of cracking. "Of course she misses you, lovey. She just had a lot of details she needed to tell us."

"She'd be here right this minute if she could," Mike said. "It'll take her a bit to get home, but getting to come home to you will be the best part of all this."

Cody nodded and burrowed further into Ellen's embrace. "I know. Mom and me have to be apart right now."

"For a little longer," Ellen said.

"But you and Danny don't have to, Uncle Mike. If you

figure out your 'adult stuff,' then you and Danny could be friends again."

Mike couldn't help but smile at Cody's innocence. "It's not so simple."

"Why?"

"Yes, Michael, why?" Ellen said.

"We're in different towns…" The excuse came out weak. *And even without that distance, he doesn't want to share his whole self with me.* Mike didn't know how to articulate it to his mom, especially in front of his impressionable nephew.

"A hundred miles is not the same as a hemisphere," his mom said.

True…

No. He couldn't be hopeful. Their time together had been a fantasy. And calling Danny tonight, using the man as a crutch to process his emotions, wasn't a good idea, no matter how much the one thing with the power to make him feel better right now would be to hear Danny's voice.

Except it might make all the difference.

Maybe he'd call on his break. A quick connection to make it possible to get through his shift without losing his hold on his emotions.

No matter what he and Danny decided to do, it wasn't going to involve them living in the same place. He'd have to get used to phone calls being enough.

Chapter Nineteen

Daniel hovered in his parents' living room, standing on the edge of his siblings' beautiful chaos with a bottle of lager Ryan had passed him. Given the spectacular fashion with which his sisters had left Bronco out of high school and college, having them back in town still shocked Daniel. Their return proved the power of forgiveness, of love, and he was going to cling to that because damn, he was going to need both those things himself tonight.

Allison was, of course, in Seattle with Rowan, but both Eloise and Charlotte had agreed to bring their families for dinner when Imogen had called around, asking them all over to celebrate the end of branding season. With living on the Triple T, Ryan and Gabrielle, along with Seth, had a much shorter commute than their sisters.

Charlotte held her infant daughter, Clara, in her arms. The pair, along with two of Charlotte's three step kids were jammed on one of the couches, in the midst of a fit of giggles. Clara's were the loudest, which was hilarious. Daniel hadn't realized how contagious baby laughs were. No doubt Billy was somewhere nearby, given how attached Charlotte was to the high-school sweetheart she'd given up and then fallen for all over again. Usually they were a family of six, but Billy's oldest, Branson, was off at college.

Charlotte wasn't the only Taylor sister who was smitten

with her new husband. Eloise sprawled with her toddling daughter on the floor, both playing under the tender eye of her husband, Dante Sanchez. His sister had shocked the town when she'd unexpectedly returned to Bronco, a month and a half away from giving birth. Her whirlwind romance with the handsome teacher had been an equal surprise, but the two were meant for each other. And Dante being a great father to little Merry wasn't a shock at all, given his profession.

A pang of longing hit Daniel. Dante didn't know it—he hadn't been present at the infamous family Thanksgiving dinner—but Eloise talking about Dante and his profession had been one of the catalysts to get Daniel thinking about breaking away from the Taylor expectations. The reminder of how he'd once dreamed of being a teacher in his youth—combined with his father's behavior the same night—had jolted him to the possibility of living his life the way he wanted to.

Well, tonight he was going to put his realizations to the test.

Partly for the sake of finding greater fulfillment at work, but more to prove he could live his life holistically, not as broken pieces.

Also, Charlotte and Eloise were proving to be wonderful parents, despite having been raised by a callous father.

Maybe there was hope for Daniel yet. Cody had seemed unfazed by Daniel's rookie attempts to connect while in Tenacity. And going off the effusive thank-you Ellen had texted on her grandson's behalf around ten minutes ago, the boy was thrilled with the present from the dinosaur museum.

Kind of odd to get a text from Mike's mom, but Mike had mentioned he was working at the club for a lot of the weekend. Still, Daniel felt uneasy. Was there something holding Mike back from reaching out?

He tipped his chin at Dante. "I played some trivia with your cousins in Tenacity last weekend. Diego and Nina?"

Dante nodded but didn't drag his loving gaze away from

Daniel's sister and niece. "Yeah, on my dad's side. Lord knows between my family and Eloise's, we're swimming in relatives."

"Big enough that our families were bound to connect at some point. And given it happened because you and Eloise found each other, I'm glad it did," Daniel said.

"Thanks," Dante replied. "It's wild how fast I went from being single to having a wife and daughter, but I wouldn't change a moment of it for anything. Merry is my heart, and Eloise is my soul, and I'm a lucky man."

Daniel smiled. His sister deserved that kind of love.

And so do I.

"We don't get to control the timing, do we?" Daniel said. "It just *happens*."

Eloise joined them, her arms full of a cheerful Merry. "Ooh, I heard you had news. In fact, I thought you might bring your 'news' with you tonight."

"I want to try to keep him, not have him run away," he joked, then sobered. "But yeah, I'd like to, though I worry."

"Our big Thanksgiving blowout still sticks with you, too?"

"I wish it didn't. Dad said awful things—to almost every single one of us—but it's been over a year."

"Oh, and he's been supportive and caring since then?"

"No. But his rigidity doesn't mean the rest of us can't be closer than we have been, despite the example he set. We can still support and love each other." He could see it was ironic to suggest this right before he planned to announce he was taking a step back from the ranch. "Since you moved back to Bronco and married Dante, and with Allison and Charlotte both finding love—"

"And us," Ryan said, sidling up to the group, his hand firmly linked in his wife Gabrielle's.

She smiled softly at her husband's claim.

"Yes, all you younglings," Daniel teased. The age gap between him and his youngest siblings didn't make as much of a difference now, but it was hard to break the habit of feeling markedly older. Then again, it didn't matter with Mike, so it shouldn't matter with anyone else, either. "We weren't close when we were growing up. Beyond, too. But we're getting there now."

"That's good for our generation, but I can't accept Dad not fully accepting *you*," Eloise said.

"Neither can I, nor should we," Daniel said. "And I need more from him than a half-assed conversation acknowledging I'm gay before I trust him or forgive him. But some of us have tried leaving, and the distance hurt us more in the long run. As much as a stiff boundary with Dad is an option, it means losing too much of the other things we love. Containment works better than severing for me."

"Well, when you're ready to bring your man by, I will welcome him with open arms," Eloise assured him.

"Thanks. Tonight wasn't the night." Daniel shook his head. The last thing he needed was for his dad to assume his decision to need time away from Taylor Beef was for Mike's sake, not Daniel's. "We'll have to do a siblings-only get-together at my place first. And maybe I'll take him to lunch with Mom."

"You want to do right by him."

"Cherish him, more like. His nephew, too." He rubbed the back of his neck. "The Coopers are close knit, and Mike is his nephew's guardian at the moment."

"Oh, Daniel, you're in it, aren't you?" Eloise looked too happy at the prospect.

"I'd say I'm sinking into the quicksand, but that makes it sound like a bad thing. And this has the possibility to be so, so good. I *want* to be in it."

In Mike's arms, his heart. His family.

He could create the space in his life to make that happen. He had the resources to detach from the parts of being a Taylor that didn't serve him anymore, while still keeping the soul-deep, important connections. It was just going to take the courage to do it.

"He bought the nephew a stack of presents at some dinosaur museum," came a helpful voice from behind them.

Seth joined the group with a sly look on his face.

"Aww, super sweet, Daniel," Eloise said.

"Cody's a great kid." He scrubbed his hands down his face. "I didn't know what else to do."

Worry struck, nearly choking him.

"Will Mike think I'm trying to buy Cody's attention?" he asked.

"Were you?" Seth replied.

"No, I was aiming to make him smile. He loves anything paleontology related. I don't… I don't want to be like Dad was when we were kids."

"I don't remember Dad ever paying attention to our interests, let alone picking up presents for us on a work trip. We never lacked anything material, but it was always Mom doing the shopping, not Dad. Nor could he have told you if one of us liked dinosaurs."

"Well, according to Cody's grandmother's text, the kid loved what I picked out." Daniel pulled out his phone and pulled up the picture Ellen had sent with the boy's thanks. Cody's wide smile filled the screen as he proudly held up a model-building kit in one hand and a dinosaur-themed board game in the other.

"Oh, my gosh," Eloise exclaimed. "First—he's adorable. And second—you're showing us *kid* pictures. *Daniel*."

"It's not like he's mine," he demurred. "Or even Mike's."

"He matters, though," Ryan said. "So does the guy. And we don't want you to be alone. How can we help?"

Air gusted from his lungs at his siblings' support. "Back me up with Dad, okay?"

Soon after, dinner was served. Lina, his parents' housekeeper and cook, had outdone herself with both the roast and vegetable dishes.

With Charlotte's and Billy's nods, their two high-school age kids, Jill and Nicky, took their loaded plates and cutlery and darted out of the room.

Daniel blinked. Had he actually just seen that? "Uh, Mom?"

She gave him a placid look. "They'll have more fun eating in front of the TV in the rec room."

His jaw dropped.

"Oh, don't look so shocked, Daniel. I'm not that out of touch. I remember how boring family dinners can be for kids."

"What happened to meals being about teaching manners?" Seth asked his mother, his eyes narrowed.

"They already have fine manners," Imogen said, her lips pursed as she cut into a roasted baby potato.

Shaking his head, Daniel dug into his own food.

Thaddeus grilled Daniel and Seth about the properties they'd seen. Imogen fussed over Clara, who was drowsing in the crook of Billy's arm, and at Merry, who was busy mashing small pieces of potato on the tray of her high chair. The happy grandmother not-so-subtly hinted at wanting more grandkids in the future, if any of her children wanted to humor her.

Dinner was going well enough that he was reluctant to change the subject to his revelations. When was the last time they'd shared a meal without fireworks?

His phone buzzed in his pocket.

Putting down his cutlery, he pulled his cell out to the side of his lap with the intent of silencing it. Mike's name was on the screen.

Oh, good grief, he'd been waiting all week for an actual call, and it came now?

His mom hated it when anyone answered their phone at the table, but screw it. He wasn't passing up the chance to hear Mike's voice.

He rose from the table. "Sorry, everyone, but I need to answer this."

Sliding his thumb across the screen, he made for the kitchen, answering as he passed under the archway between the rooms.

"Hey, Michael," he said.

"Uh, hey." A sigh followed, strong enough to take the leaves off a tree. "I'm on my break at the Social Club, and I needed to hear your voice."

He settled against one of the counters. "I've been waiting for you to call."

"I tried not to, but…"

Damn, he'd been right to assume something was off. "Are you okay?"

"I am. Maggie isn't. She's coming home."

Daniel's gut twisted. "Oh, damn, she's that sick? When you texted me about her still not feeling well, it didn't sound that serious."

"Yeah. She tried to convince us it wasn't, until she couldn't avoid it anymore." Mike ran through the description of a parasitic illness and the treatment involved and all the steps his sister was going to have to take to get home, including Ellen flying down to help Maggie get home.

"Did you tell Cody?" Daniel asked, his heart aching for all of them.

"Yeah." Mike sounded so damn broken. "He's worried about her. Excited to see her earlier than expected, too. So long as we can get through some days without my mom."

"What's that going to look like?"

"My dad and I will have to have Cody with us in the barn or on the range sometimes. And I'll be leaning on Jenna for babysitting in the afternoons and evenings for my bartending shifts."

"No." The need to step in swamped him. "Lean on me."

"How? You're back to work."

"I'm upper management. I have some flexibility with when I can be in the office or working remotely, even." Soon he'd have a hell of a lot more leeway, but not in time to pitch in for the Coopers. "I can drive back and forth to Tenacity on your work nights."

"That's a three-hour round trip."

"I want to support you. And I know your family needs you to keep up your work at the Social Club," he said, knowing Mike's candle was a mere nub from being burned at both ends. Maybe if Daniel had some time to work with Larry, he could help the Coopers improve their bottom line and, in turn, ease the pressure on Mike. He was excited to have the opportunity to explore those kinds of options—once he officially took his leave from Taylor Beef.

"I do." Mike groaned. "Mom flying down to Maggie doesn't qualify for an emergency booking, so you wouldn't believe the price of the plane ticket."

Daniel could solve that dilemma with the click of a button. "I have enough airline points to more than cover both their flights."

Silence.

"Mike?"

"I wasn't complaining about it as a back-asswards attempt at getting you to pay for it," Mike finally said.

"I didn't think you were—not at all." What he *wanted* to do was pull out his platinum card and cover the cost of a private charter for both Ellen and Maggie, but if air miles set Mike off, no way would he accept something costlier. "You care for everyone around you. I want to be the one who cares for you. And this is one small way I can alleviate some of your stress."

A noise of frustration grumbled across the connection. "I don't want to even start this pattern."

"I don't see a pattern."

"Not yet, but if you always offer to cover costs, it could."

"It's not money. It's airline points."

"It's all currency."

Daniel took a deep breath. If he bowled Mike over by insisting on doing what he thought was best, he'd be veering way too close to the Thaddeus Taylor School of Thought. "Okay. I hear you. I promise it's a no-strings offer. Every part of me wants to make your life easier. But if it stresses you out more to accept monetary help, then I won't push."

Another long pause.

Daniel wanted to fill the silent seconds with pleas, but Mike needed the processing time.

"I'll think about it," Mike conceded, then exhaled. It sounded like he was barely able to take in a breath.

Daniel wanted to climb through the damn phone and collect Mike, help him carry his burdens.

"I'm so sorry this is happening," he said.

"I should get back to the bar."

"Okay. Want to call me after your shift?" Daniel offered.

"It'll be late." His voice was rough, like he was trying to hold off his emotions. No doubt he didn't want to get choked up at work.

"I'll be up," Daniel promised.

"Right. Okay. I'll call."

When Daniel made his way back into the dining room, all eyes were on him. Each face around the table, save his father's, wore varying degrees of curiosity, from Seth's bemused interest to Eloise's mischievous fascination. His dad's expression was more neutral, but Daniel would take it, considering how often Thaddeus ranged from insensitive to downright harsh.

Eloise leaned forward. "How's *Michael*, big brother?"

Daniel shook his head. "Were you holding that in the entire time I was in the kitchen?"

"I won rock, paper, scissors for who got to harass you first," she said.

Glancing at his parents, he waited for the inevitable scolding for even mildly childish behavior at the dinner table.

Imogen offered up a mild *tsk*. "*Not* that I want to get into a habit of you all answering your phones at the table, but tell us about your man, Daniel."

His father flinched.

Oh, God. Here it goes. His pulse pounded in his throat.

"He's a rancher in Tenacity," he croaked.

Frowning, his dad said, "But you live here."

"I do. And Mike lives a hell of a drive away. These are facts."

"Why bother? This life doesn't allow for that kind of distance. Waste of time, if you ask me," Thaddeus announced.

"Not that I did ask you, but it isn't a waste of time at all," Daniel said calmly. "And it's pushed me to make some changes. Starting next week, I'm going to be shifting more decisions over to my senior director."

"You're my oldest son, Daniel. That means something when you're a Taylor." Thaddeus's tone darkened. "Including honoring your responsibilities."

"It should mean something—like love with no strings and a safe place to land and launch again. *Asking* your children to contribute, not guilting them into sacrificing their own dreams to fulfill your own."

"You want to talk sacrifices, son? You think your mother and I haven't sacrificed for you and your brothers and sisters?"

Daniel took a deep breath. "I know you did. But I also know that I came out at twenty, and two years ago you still hadn't clued in to what that means. More than one thing can be true at once, Dad. And some of the things we've accepted are wrong and need to be changed."

His father's expression grew stormy, a look Daniel recognized all too well. "What kind of changes?"

"For you? You'll have to answer that question yourself. For me, I can't keep tucking parts of myself away. I'm tired. And lonely, until I met Mike and he blew the top off the little box I've jammed myself into. And I'm going to take the time I need to evaluate what *I* want, independent of Taylor Beef."

Anger snapped in his father's gaze. "After everything I've given to you kids—"

"Thaddeus." Imogen gripped her napkin in both hands. "We raised independent, fierce souls. They've been busy making their mark on the world, the same as you have. And it's time to accept that what drives you doesn't always drive them. You pushed the girls away, and we're lucky they made their way back home. I'm not willing to stand by while the same thing happens with Daniel."

Her watery smile landed on Daniel.

Thaddeus sat at the head of the table and stewed. "He's my *son*, Imogen, and for him to sit here…"

"Dad, take a breath," Eloise warned as she tried to distract her daughter with a few tiny pieces of carrot and roast. "Not only are you going to upset the little ones, but Daniel more than deserves to be heard."

Daniel's stomach churned, fighting the few bits of food he'd managed to swallow. Was this discussion even worth it? Should he have bothered trying? Maybe they were too entrenched to change or heal the dynamic that had caused so much pain over time.

No. I need to say my piece. Getting my family life sorted is part of being "all in."

"I am your son." His voice was shaking. Oh, well. "But more importantly, I'm my own person."

"Do you have a plan?" his mother prodded.

"Not yet. I'm going to take a leave of absence to give myself time to *make* a plan. There are a number of struggling ranches around Tenacity in need of fair advice. Including Cooper Ranch. I like the idea of doing some independent consultant work."

"So you're leaving Taylor Beef over a *fling*?" his dad blustered.

"Mike is not a fling. Also, consider him an inspiration, not a reason. I'm doing this for me. But am I considering the potential for a life in Tenacity? Yeah."

With any luck, Mike would accept his efforts as proof he could change.

"That's not how this works, Daniel," his dad said between gritted teeth. "Going back generations, fathers worked themselves into the ground to pass their legacy on to their sons, and the sons pick up the mantle when it's time."

"And now we're questioning that, Dad," Ryan interjected. "It's messed up for so many reasons."

"Is that true, Seth?" Thaddeus said.

Seth nodded. "Even though I know it was painful for Charlotte and Eloise—Allison, too—to cut ties for a while in order to find what makes them happy, sometimes I'm jealous they had the guts to do it. And I think you're damn lucky they're still willing to sit at this table with you. Daniel, too, given you continue to ignore who he is at his core."

Their dad glanced around the table, from one happy couple to the next. Charlotte and Billy. Eloise and Dante. Ryan and Gabrielle. Frustration, and his own measure of exhaustion, weighed at the corners of his mouth. "I know I'm stubborn. The Triple T requires it. But I can accept when I need to do some reconsidering."

It wasn't an apology, but it was more progress than Daniel had seen his dad make in a long time. He wasn't going to fool himself into believing Thaddeus would be able to meaningfully shift his perspective in the span of a few minutes.

"Home *matters*, Dad," Daniel said. "That's why I wanted

to have this conversation instead of just putting my assistant in charge and leaving."

Seth spoke up next to Daniel. "I can see why Tenacity fascinates you. It needs an influx of cash, but there's something special about it."

"There is. And about Mike, too," Daniel said. "He made me see how much I keep my life segmented and separate. And I need to stop."

"You are quite private, dear," Imogen said carefully.

"I've had to be." Daniel shot a look at his dad. Thaddeus was too stone faced to read. "I care for Mike. I want to make room for him in my life. Part of which is me eventually bringing him into our family and you acknowledging how he means the damn world to me and treating him accordingly. Even if it doesn't make sense to you."

Silence hung like a cloud over the table.

"When I was young, we never aired family laundry at the dinner table," Thaddeus grumbled.

"And you are worse off for it," Eloise said.

"Families share important things with each other, Dad," Charlotte said, leaning into Billy's side to accept his one-armed squeeze.

Daniel nodded. "And Mike has a lot going on with *his* family right now. Somehow I need to convince him to let me help with getting his mom to South America."

He quickly explained Maggie's situation and the offer he'd extended to cover the plane tickets.

"If he won't take your air miles, he can have mine," Eloise said. "I have more than I'll ever use."

"Thanks. I'll see what help he's willing to accept," Daniel said.

"Your—" Imogen cocked her head. "Are you calling him your boyfriend yet, dear?"

Oh god, had he and Mike even left things in the place where the label applied?

He shrugged.

"Little old for 'boyfriend,' aren't you?" his dad groused.

"Mike isn't," Seth said under his breath, nudging Daniel with an elbow. "He's younger than Ryan, even."

"You can shut up, now," Daniel said between gritted teeth.

"How young?" Thaddeus asked.

"Does it matter?" Daniel shot back.

His dad laid his cutlery on the edges of his plate. "It does if your...er, your—"

"Partner?" Daniel supplied.

His father jerked out a nod. "Right. Your *partner* needs to understand your priorities."

"Mike understands me better than you ever have, Dad," Daniel said.

"Well," Thaddeus blustered. "That's probably true."

Imogen sent him a pointed look. "And why is that, dear?"

"Because I didn't try. And I should have done better." He stared back at his wife. "There. Promise fulfilled."

"In part," she said mildly.

Daniel would have said something, too, but his jaw was resting on top of his slice of prime rib.

Had his dad ever alluded to wrongdoing about anything?

It wasn't nearly enough to make up for the years of hurt. Daniel didn't know if he'd ever get to the point where he could fully forgive his father. But it was enough to feel justified to keep sitting at the family table, for the sake of his relationship with his mother and siblings and their families.

"Did you almost *apologize*?" Eloise asked their dad.

"No, he didn't," Imogen said. "Which means he still has work to do. After the last time this happened at our dinner table, I made him promise he would."

Their dad lifted a hand in a *stop* motion. "I am. I will."

"I hope that's true," Daniel said quietly.

Thaddeus cleared his throat. "If their spread is short on hands, we can spare two or three for a couple of weeks."

Everyone stared at his abrupt subject change.

"Uh, who do you mean?" Daniel asked.

"Your frie—er, partner. And his family. Ranching doesn't stop for illness. We're all familiar with it being a three-hundred-sixty-five-days-a-year undertaking. If they're needing to take time off because his sister is sick and it would help to send hands from the Triple T, we can do that."

Disbelief churned through Daniel. "Really? For strangers?"

"They aren't strangers to you," his dad replied.

No, they weren't.

Daniel didn't know what to do with his dad's offer. He didn't want to be in a position where he owed Thaddeus anything. He didn't want to give off the impression the small acknowledgment had wiped their slate clean, either.

"I'll have to ask the Coopers what works best for them," he managed to choke out.

"Talk to them, and if it's a yes, I'll have people in Tenacity by midweek next week."

"Okay," Daniel said. "Mike was adamant they could go it alone, but I have to help in some way."

"Think about what he *does* want, Dan," Eloise encouraged, sending Dante a brief, adoring smile. "If he's hurting, give him more of what he *will* accept."

Me. He'll accept me.

I have to get back to him.

And not in a few weeks. Not when they had all the answers, but in the middle of their mess.

Now.

He pushed back his chair. "Mom, I'm sorry. I need to cut out early."

Mike needed not to feel alone when he got home from work tonight, and if Daniel hit the road soon, he could be there before the Social Club closed.

Chapter Twenty

Mike gripped the steering wheel, his headlights flashing along tufts of wild grass and the seemingly endless fence of the access road on Cooper Ranch.

He knew it wasn't endless. He drove it most days. But the darkness stole perspective, and the drive always seemed longer at night.

Back in senior year, he and Maggie had hiked it on foot, stumbling the entire half mile after getting deposited on the main road by their designated driver. One night he'd even piggybacked her when one of her heels had broken earlier in the evening. By the time he'd gotten to the circle drive between the house and the barns, his thighs had been screaming.

He hadn't let her down, though.

The endpoint—getting his sister home safe—had kept him going. It still did. Every exhausted morning. Every hour behind the bar.

And especially now, with her sick and alone in a foreign country.

And I'm so damn tired of knowing that the credit card bill from a last-minute plane flight could be what puts us under this month.

Of course, if he agreed to Danny's offer...

He shook his head. There was always going to be something. A plane flight this month could be a new truck transmission next month or an increase in feed prices.

And no matter what it was, his parents got through it by leaning on each other.

God, why had he sent Danny away, or at least suggested they needed space? It was the opposite of what he wanted right now.

Turning down the side lane to his own house, he wanted to slap himself upside the head for pushing away the one person who was willing and able to take on some of the weight of Mike's world.

If he hadn't been stubborn and scared, would he be driving toward a warm bed tonight?

He steered past the copse of trees and nearly slammed on the brakes in surprise.

Why was there a car in his driveway? A sleek Audi he'd never seen before, shining in the moonlight.

And the driver, lounging on the porch swing, long legs propped on the top of the rail and crossed at the ankle.

Mike had forgotten to leave his front light on. The small glow of a cell phone screen cast a blue tint across a handsome face.

Somehow Mike parked and made his way to the porch, all but stumbling into Danny's offered embrace as he rose. It lasted for minutes, until he finally got his feet under him. Two strong hands cupped his cheeks, tethering him to the ground, making sure he didn't float away from the shock.

"You're here."

"There was nowhere else I wanted to be, Mike. I can't imagine you coming home to an empty house tonight." Thumbs stroked along his cheeks, bringing feeling into his face for the first time all night. "Damn. Did I misinterpret? You've got your family. You're not alone. You calling me doesn't mean you need me here—"

"Hey, stop." Sliding his arms around Danny's waist, Mike fell into the other man. His face was buried in Danny's neck, like the warm skin and soft cashmere was a charging station and Mike was down to 3 percent battery. "I need you here. I *want* you here. You being here is the best part of my day."

"I wasn't sure." Danny's words rumbled in his chest, against Mike's cheek. "You were clear you needed space, but then you called, and with Maggie's news… I needed to see you, to make sure you were okay."

"I'm better now," Mike said.

And he was. For so long, he'd been the one to offer up his shoulder to the people around him, but now he'd found one strong enough to rest on himself, and damn, he needed to stop being so stubborn and accept it.

"Do you have to go back tonight?" Mike asked.

"No." Strong palms pressed between his shoulder blades and his spine right at his waist. "I'll drive back early Monday morning, if that works." A long pause. "I'm hoping to be able to talk to your parents tomorrow. With your stamp of approval, of course."

"About what?"

"Maggie coming home. Of all people, my dad wants to pitch in."

"You told your dad?"

"You called during dinner. More importantly, I answered. Can't get away with interrupting a meal without giving up some information."

A lump rose in Mike's throat. "Still being stingy with relationship information with them?"

Danny let out a dry chuckle.

"It's okay. I can't expect everyone to be as close to their family as I am to mine, and—"

"Mike." Danny rocked back, breaking their contact. He jammed his hands into his pockets. "I opened up about more than I ever have. With explaining what was happening with Maggie, I kept it to basic details. But my dad… He offered to help. I can understand if you don't want to accept. Hell, I almost turned him down given how often he's chosen to ignore who I am and who I love. But this could make a meaningful difference for you and your parents. He'll send a couple of ranch hands to work with Harold, which would allow you and your dad to take some time off to help with Maggie's return and recovery if you want."

"Triple T employees?"

"Yeah. Whether it's genuine generosity or an attempt to show me he cares, I don't know. It's foreign from him, to be honest."

"It's a big offer. And add in the air miles…"

Danny smiled. "We could upgrade them to business class. It would make Maggie's journey home a hell of a lot easier."

"Yeah." He sighed. "I was looking at it in terms of my pride, but it isn't about me. Maggie's health is the priority."

"Plus, you might not hear the end of it from your mom if she finds out she had to squish into economy instead of getting a fully reclining seat."

Mike laughed. Probably for the first time in twelve hours, and damn, it felt good.

"I want my twin home," he said. "And healthy. She'd be so much more comfortable, and with the extra hands from your dad, we'll be able to take care of her once she's here."

"I can call the airline in the morning," Danny said.

"We can tell my parents then, too." He cleared his throat and nuzzled back against Danny's neck. "And I get to wake up with your head on the pillow next to mine. God, that sounds perfect."

"I want waking up with you to be our usual, Mike."

"How?"

The earnestness in Danny's dark gaze nearly bowled him over. "I've never felt like this about anyone before. You light up my world."

"I feel the same way," Mike said, stealing a kiss. Slow and easy, with the promise of flaring hot the second they weren't standing on the porch. "But I also feel a whole lot of life pressing on me from all sides."

"And I want to stand next to you while you face those things. Be your sounding board. Support you while you make your way through the next few weeks and months and beyond."

"Beyond, huh?" Mike said.

"Yeah."

"Will you share the ways your life is overwhelming, too? I don't expect you to tear down all the boundaries you have—they keep you safe—but I want to be safe enough for you not to need them with me. And for the parts of your life where you can include me, that you do. And for the parts you can't, that we have an open conversation about why."

"Yes. But I don't only want to share the easy parts. I—" Danny exhaled, puffing out his lips like he'd been holding his breath. "I'm taking a leave of absence from work for the summer."

Mike blinked. "What?"

"I've been working up to it, and it's what I need. Time to explore if I want my own spread or to stay with Taylor Beef or if I want to help others—ranchers like your dad—maximize what they have so that they don't lose their livelihoods."

"Your own spread?" Mike swallowed, resisting the tension in his throat. "I thought you gave up on North Dakota."

He was counting on that decision.

"I did. It's way too far from home. I'd be looking closer, if at all." Danny let go of Mike's waist with one hand and rubbed the back of his own neck, his expression turning sheepish and nervous all at once. "Would you consider it too much if I live in Tenacity while I'm figuring that out?"

The world started buzzing. "Wh-where in Tenacity?"

"I'd rent a place," Danny said. "Cody's life is going to

change enough without adding me to the chaos. Nor would I ask you to share space this quickly. But it sure would be nice to be a quick drive away from each other."

Would it ever...

A low sound escaped the back of Mike's throat, all the relief and need and joy from having this man here and willing to look to the future together.

"That's not a yes, sweetheart," Danny said.

"Because I can't quite believe you're here, saying all these things."

"I am here. And as much as I'm not cutting ties with Bronco—I want to introduce you to the rest of my siblings and my mom, and even my dad if he's truly starting to change—I want to stay here for a few months. To find out everything there is to know about you and Cody and Cooper Ranch and Tenacity during the summer. To get to know Maggie, too, once she's home and well."

"You... You're including Cody as part of your equation. My family, too. And I love that," he said, all of a sudden remembering the present Cody had opened earlier today. "The dinosaur, the board game—thank you so much. You really listened to him."

"He's an easy kid to read. And even though Maggie is coming back, I know you're always going to be a father figure for him. Which means, as long as I'm not reading this wrong, whoever you're dating will be important to him, too."

"A hundred percent." Mike stroked a hand down the faint stubble on Danny's cheek. "Anyone who's with me will be part of Cody's life."

"Is it okay that I'm terrified and excited all at once?"

"I'd think you were doing it wrong if you weren't."

Danny chuckled.

"You just want to spend the summer together, then?" Mike asked. A few months wasn't forever...

A line of kisses landed along his jaw. "Fall sounds good, too. There's a harvest festival in Bronco I could take you to. And then come winter, I could drag you away skiing for a week. Spending Christmas together, with our families. And my fly-fishing could use some definite attention come spring-time." He pulled back, his expression growing serious. "I want to share my life with you, Mike. I love you. I want to be able to say it every day and share space and life's most important moments with you. I—please."

"Yes," he said in a voice hoarse with emotion. It had never been easier to agree to something.

Danny drew back. "Yes to everything?"

Mike nodded. "I can't imagine anything better than spending the next while falling further in love with you."

Strong arms pulled him in. "I've been waiting my life to feel the way you make me feel. Once I've given you my heart, I don't plan to ask for it back, Michael Cooper."

"Good." Mike grinned and laid a kiss on Danny, hoping for a lifetime of them to follow. "Because I plan on keeping it."

Epilogue

Daniel leaned a shoulder against the doorway of the primary ensuite of the Bronco Heights house and smiled like an absolute fool. His fiancé was staring in the mirror, fidgeting with the collar of his Western-style shirt and then the few stray curls on his forehead.

Who knew it was possible to be so damn *soft* for another person? He'd love Mike for every second they were given on this earth.

A couple of days ago, right after they'd decorated the Christmas tree in the Cooper Ranch house where they now lived 90 percent of the time, Daniel had gotten down on one knee. And because Daniel was the luckiest man in existence, Mike had said "yes."

"Sweetheart?" he said.

Mike startled, clearly having been lost enough in his worries not to notice Daniel's presence. "Oh, geez. Is it time to go?"

"Almost. And you look damn good. Too good for a two-year-old's birthday party."

Good enough that Daniel promised himself he'd be undoing all the buttons of that shirt once they got home.

"It's hard not to think Eloise's standards will be high, given she's been planning this thing for over a month."

"She has," Daniel said with a laugh, "but it's still going to be casual. I have a feeling the guest-of-honor will end the party with cake in her hair."

Eloise and Dante were hosting their daughter's second-birthday celebration for an ever-expanding list of family and friends. Daniel knew his sister had gone over the top with the cake. She'd special-ordered a massive creation, animal themed in a nod to Merry's love for anything on four legs.

"Besides—" closing the distance between them, Daniel slid one hand around Mike's waist and pushed the last couple of stubborn curls into place with the other "—I like you a little disheveled."

"I'll show you disheveled." Mouth tilted in a teasing smirk, Mike leaned in, an inch from Daniel's own. He threaded his fingers through Daniel's hair. "If you want me to, that is."

"I always want you," he said.

Mike groaned. "Corny, babe. You're twisting my words."

"Just telling the truth." He closed the last inch between them and kissed his fiancé until a moan rumbled at the back of Mike's throat.

After a long minute, Mike broke the kiss, regret darkening his handsome face.

"I should take this off." Mike twisted his engagement ring around his finger. "It's not right to show up to someone else's party and steal the show with big news."

"Sweetheart. The birthday girl isn't going to remember a moment of this day. I don't think she's going to mind if she has to share the stage for a few minutes. You agreed to spend the rest of your life with me. My family will want to celebrate that with us. Yours certainly did."

There had been no hiding the engagement from the Coopers, not when Mike had bounded out of the house the morning after the proposal, looking like Danny had wrangled the stars for him.

Daniel had purposefully proposed a week *after* Thanksgiving, so that they could get through the minefield of a holiday first. He hadn't wanted to risk tainting their engagement announcement by delivering it at his parents' dinner table. Especially not during a holiday with a fraught history like Thanksgiving at the Triple T.

Mike had joined the Taylors for the holiday, though. Daniel's siblings and mom had spent enough time with Mike by now that they'd absorbed him into the fold like any other Taylor partner. It hadn't been a relaxed night, exactly, but it had at least been…neutral. Enough that Daniel and Mike had been able to laugh about the handful of awkward moments with Thaddeus once they'd retreated to their own house.

Their Thanksgiving meal at Ellen and Larry's, delayed by a day to make sure they hadn't needed to pick one family over the other, had been a hundred times more chill.

The most important part was that they'd shared both nights together, hand-in-hand for a lot of the time.

Hell, they had countless meals and family events in the future to look forward to. Maybe one day they'd decide to welcome a child of their own into their life, would be ordering a cake and throwing a birthday party for their own two-year-old.

His pulse skittered at the thought.

"Hey," Mike said, stroking Daniel's cheek with his thumb. "Lost you for a minute. You okay? Are *you* nervous?"

"No, I'm better than good." His voice was rough, though. He still got a little choked up at the possibilities of what life might bring with this wonderful, caring man.

Mike's brows furrowed. "You sure?"

"I, uh…" He wiped a palm down his face. "Drifted ahead in time, a little. Beyond our engagement and wedding. *Other* toddler birthdays."

"Other…*oh*."

"Yeah." He smiled sheepishly. "It's pretty easy to picture. The more time I spend with the kids in our life—Cody, of course, but Merry, too, and Charlotte's brood—the more I can see how amazing it would be to do that with you. *But* I don't want to rush anything. You only just agreed to be my husband. Which still feels like a damn miracle."

"Yeah. I want to savor this part, Danny." Mike pressed another kiss to his mouth, gentle this time. "I like the freedom we have, now that Maggie is home and healthy and doesn't need as much help with Cody. And with you pitching in half time for my folks and consulting the rest of the week—I'm selfish. I want all your free hours to myself for now."

"You want to skip the party, then?" he said with a wink.

"No! We spent eons searching for the right stuffed dog. I want to see her open it."

"I still say we should have gotten Merry a real puppy," Daniel joked.

"Daniel Cooper, you wouldn't."

"Of course not. Not for her birthday." He nipped at the sensitive spot below Mike's ear. "For Christmas, though—"

"Not then, either!"

He swallowed Mike's outrage with a heated kiss, one that would for sure make them late. Hopefully, the engagement ring on Mike's finger would ease his mother's and sister's inevitable annoyed reactions.

Daniel pressed his fiancé against the sink and made an absolute mess of him. Loving and wanting the man in his arms used up almost all of Daniel's brain cells, but the one or two free ones were stuck contemplating a puppy. He wouldn't get one for his niece for Christmas, of course.

What about for Mike, though?

Every rancher needed a dog, and Cody would love it and they had space in both their houses…

Yeah. Once they got back from the birthday festivities and returned to Tenacity, he'd explore the rescues available there.

So many possibilities. The best part of it all? Any direction he and Mike chose to take together would be filled with love.

* * * * *

Don't miss the next installment of the new continuity
Montana Mavericks: The Tenacity Social Club

Maverick's Full House
by USA TODAY *bestselling author Tara Taylor Quinn*
On sale June 2025, wherever Harlequin books
and ebooks are sold.

And look for the previous books in the series,

The Maverick's Promise
by Melissa Senate

A Maverick's Road Home
by USA TODAY *bestselling author Catherine Mann*

All in with the Maverick
by Elizabeth Hrib

Available now!